CRITICAL A[...]
THE WOR[...]
JAMES RADA, JR.

Battlefield Angels

"Rada describes women religious who selflessly performed life-saving work in often miserable conditions and thereby gained the admiration and respect of countless contemporaries. In so doing, Rada offers an appealing narrative and an entry point into the wealth of sources kept by the sisters."

Catholic News Service

Between Rail and River

"The book is an enjoyable, clean family read, with characters young and old for a broad-based appeal to both teens and adults. *Between Rail and River* also provides a unique, regional appeal, as it teaches about a particular group of people, ordinary working 'canawlers' in a story that goes beyond the usual coverage of life during the Civil War."

Historical Fiction Review

Canawlers

"A powerful, thoughtful and fascinating historical novel, *Canawlers* documents author James Rada, Jr. as a writer of considerable and deftly expressed storytelling talent."

Midwest Book Review

"James Rada, of Cumberland, has written a historical novel for high-schoolers and adults, which relates the adventures, hardships and ultimate tragedy of a family of boaters on the C&O Canal. … The tale moves quickly and should hold the attention of readers looking for an imaginative adventure set on the canal at a critical time in history."

Along the Towpath

The Rain Man

"*The Rain Man* starts out with a bang and engages the reader with its fast-moving plot."

Beyond 50

"*The Rain Man* is a mystery thriller that races from the first raindrops that began the flooding to its dangerous climax in Wills Creek as it became a raging torrent."

Cumberland Times-News

OCTOBER MOURNING

by
James Rada, Jr.

LEGACY
PUBLISHING
A division of AIM Publishing Group

OTHER BOOKS BY JAMES RADA, JR.

Non-Fiction

Battlefield Angels: The Daughters of Charity Work as Civil War Nurses

Beyond the Battlefield: Stories from Gettysburg's Rich History

Echoes of War Drums: The Civil War in Mountain Maryland

The Last to Fall: The 1922 March, Battles & Deaths of U.S. Marines at Gettysburg

Looking Back: True Stories of Mountain Maryland

Looking Back II: More True Stories of Mountain Maryland

No North, No South: The Grand Reunion at the 50th Anniversary of the Battle of Gettysburg

Saving Shallmar: Christmas Spirit in a Coal Town

Fiction

Between Rail and River

Canawlers

Lock Ready

October Mourning

The Rain Man

For Gina Gallucci and Kelly Hinchcliffe,
the youngest old maids I know,
and two people whose friendship I treasure.

This is a work of fiction. All the characters and events portrayed in this book are either fictitious or used fictitiously.

OCTOBER MOURNING

Published by Legacy Publishing, a division of AIM Publishing Group.
Gettysburg, Pennsylvania.
Copyright © 2006 by James Rada, Jr.
All rights reserved.
Printed in the United States of America.
Second printing: June 2016.

ISBN 978-0692711750

Cover photo courtesy of Albert Feldstein

LEGACY
PUBLISHING

315 Oak Lane • Gettysburg, Pennsylvania 17325

PROLOGUE

If Sarah Jenkins had known that Wednesday morning, cool and overcast as it was, was the beginning of her last day of life, she wouldn't have gone grocery shopping at the Centre Street Market. It would have been a waste of those last few, precious hours of her twenty-seven years.

No, if she had recognized her phlegm-filled cough and flushed cheeks for the symptoms they were, she would have locked herself in her bedroom away from her family and friends. She would have spent her final hours in sadness as well as agony.

It still would have been a waste of effort, but it would have given her last day a purpose. It would have given her last day of life a sense of nobility and self-sacrifice.

For as long as she remained coherent, Sarah would have cried and prayed to God for relief from the pain. She would have written letters to her sons, telling them she knew they would grow into fine men who would marry wonderful wives and have many children to carry on the family name. She would have written a letter to her husband who was fighting in the Great War in Germany, telling him how much she loved him and how blessed she was to have spent one-third of her life with him.

Sarah would have done all this because it would have meant that her family and hundreds more in Allegany County may have lived even as she died. Or at least she would not have been the one who brought death to their homes.

She didn't know that Wednesday, September 25, 1918, was her last day of life, though.

And because she didn't, the hundreds died.

The epidemic in a rural Western Maryland county represented only a miniscule portion of forty million people felled by the Spanish Influenza pandemic of 1918. The total number who died in Allegany County paled in comparison to the more than 11,000 people who died from the flu in Philadelphia in October. The devastation certainly was-n't as great as the Eskimo villages to the far north that lost every man, woman and child, but each Allegany County victim was a person like Sarah Jenkins...someone's mother, wife, sister or daughter. Someone's father, husband, brother or son.

Each person's death brought sadness and fear to others in the community. It was the sadness of the loss of a loved one. It was the fear that the next death would be yours. Death played in the streets and flew on the breezes in the fall of 1918.

In Western Maryland, October became the month of death. It became the month of mourning.

October mourning.

WEDNESDAY, SEPTEMBER 25, 1918

Sarah Jenkins picked up the red apples stacked on the display counter at the Centre Street Market. She studied each one for bruises and felt the surface for soft spots. Bruised or soft apples went back onto the pile. If it showed a tinge of green to hint that it wasn't ripe, she set it back down. Only the reddest, firmest apples would suit her needs. Her sons loved apples, but she didn't want to choose any with bad spots. If Gregory happened to bite into one that was "mushy", more likely than not, it would wind up being thrown across the room at his brother Paul instead of being eaten.

Sarah pulled a linen handkerchief from her purse and dabbed at the sweat on her forehead. It was hot out for a fall day. The newspaper hadn't mentioned anything about the county having an Indian summer. Maybe she shouldn't have worn her winter coat for the walk to the market, but it was fall after all. It was supposed to be cool out. Now she felt overheated and the coat was unbuttoned.

Sarah picked out half a dozen fine, red apples that would pass Gregory's inspection and set them in her basket. She moved on to the oranges. The hand-lettered sign on the pile said they were fresh off the train from Florida.

The Centre Street Market was a small, family-owned store where Sarah liked to shop in since it was only two blocks from her home on Valley Street. The market had only three aisles. Shelves lined the walls holding most of the canned goods. Fresh fruits and vegetables were positioned on the aisle shelves near the front of the store because they needed to sell the quickest. The store had to have the lights on inside all of the time because the front windows were so covered with signs advertising specials and sales they nearly blocked out the sun.

John Carter, the owner of the store, stacked the Florida oranges on the counter next to the apples.

"Good morning, Mrs. Jenkins," he said, nodding to her.

"Good morning, Mr. Carter."

"How are those young ones of yours?"

Sarah smiled. "A handful. They miss their father, but they are proud of him."

Mr. Carter chuckled.

Gregory and Paul were balls of energy who wore Sarah out at times, but she loved them. Sarah considered making fresh orange juice to serve the boys Friday night. It would be a treat for them. With their father off in the army fighting the Germans somewhere in France, Sarah liked to make her sons treats to keep their minds off the Great War. Keeping herself busy also helped keep Sarah's mind off the fighting and the danger Theo was in.

She had received a letter from him yesterday, but it was a month old. He was in France and feeling tired from a battle the day before. She wasn't sure what day that was because he couldn't say. He was fine and unscathed and he dreamed of her and the boys often. The first thing he wanted to do when he came home was to eat a thick steak with a huge baked potato covered with sour cream and chives. The second thing he wanted to do was sleep in a bed and not in a cot.

Sarah prayed for Theo every morning and evening and dreamed about him every night. In between, she followed the war's progress in the *Cumberland Evening Times* and watched for her husband's name among the casualty lists. If that nightmare were to happen, she wasn't sure who would receive notice first, her or the newspaper. So far, God had answered her prayers. Her husband was still alive. Her dreams hadn't come true, though. Theo still wasn't home.

That would come. Hopefully soon. Things were going well for the Americans and there were rumors of peace talks. If true, it meant Theo might be home by the end of the year. Sarah knew she was a poor substitute for a father in her sons' hearts. Paul and Gregory missed being able to wrestle and fish with their father. They needed Theo around to emulate not a mother who was always worried they would hurt themselves when they played roughly with each other.

All the orange juice in the world couldn't replace their father.

Sarah grabbed the nearest orange to feel its firmness. She didn't want to buy any that were more peel than pulp. She brought it close to her nose and smelled the sharp tang. It was a pleasant smell, though it always made her wrinkle her nose.

4

"Where in Florida did these come from, Mr. Carter?" Sarah asked.

John Carter straightened up from his work. He rubbed his lower back. He was an older man who had been ready to retire from the business when his son was drafted to fight in the war. Now John Carter was keeping the business running until his son returned.

The strain showed. The wrinkles in his face were deeper than they had been early last year. He moved slower and his hair had turned white in the last year. Sarah could remember Mr. Carter as a young man. As a girl, she would come to the store with her mother to shop and Mr. Carter would give her a mint and a smile while her mother paid for her groceries.

"They're from somewhere down around Orlando, Mrs. Jenkins. It's a fine batch. I was told they were picked only three days ago. They just came off the train this morning," Mr. Carter replied.

Sarah nodded. "They do look fresh."

She added a dozen large oranges to her basket and then took her handkerchief out and dabbed at her forehead again.

"Don't you think it's a little hot in here, Mr. Carter?"

He laid two more oranges on the growing pile as he shook his head. "Not at all. I'm working and I haven't even broken a sweat."

His forehead was dry. It wasn't even glistening. So why could she feel perspiration rolling down the side of her face? It couldn't just be that she was wearing a coat.

"Well, look at me. I'm perspiring." Sarah pointed at her face.

John Carter studied her face for a moment. He frowned. "Your face is flushed, Mrs. Jenkins. Perhaps you had better sit down. I have a chair over behind the front counter."

He reached out to take her by the arm to lead her to the chair. Sarah wiped her forehead once more and then shook her head.

"No, thank you, I'll be fine, really. I guess I just need some fresh air. The walk home should cool me down," she said.

Mr. Carter nodded skeptically. Sarah doubted it herself. It hadn't felt any cooler outside the store. They must be heading into an Indian summer. It wasn't supposed to be this warm in late September.

Sarah smiled and moved past Mr. Carter to continue her shopping. The grocer turned to watch her walk down the aisle.

She stopped in the middle of the aisle, apparently staring at nothing. She looked like a statue caught in a pose. She was too still and her face was pale.

When she didn't move for half a minute, John Carter said, "Mrs. Jenkins?"

Sarah moaned lightly right before she collapsed to the floor.

Alan Keener heard his name called over Western Maryland Hospital's public address system. He stopped writing his patient notes and hurried out of his office to the admitting room at the end of the hall.

The Stein Funeral Home ambulance drivers brought in a young woman on a stretcher as Alan entered the room. They set the stretcher on the floor and lifted the woman gently up onto the padded examining table. The woman's skin was pale and the lights in the room gleamed off of the perspiration on her skin.

She weakly protested being moved. Her hands reached out to the two drivers. Tim McCaffrey, one of the drivers, patted her hand.

"Please, take me home. I'm fine. Really, it was just a bit of exhaustion," the woman said.

Alan knew that was a lie just by looking at her. She was too weak to sit up on her own. Her arms shook and then collapsed when she tried.

"We're only trying to make sure that you're all right, ma'am. Let the doctor decide how you are," Tim said before moving off.

"What has happened here?" Alan asked.

He went to the counter and pulled out a thermometer. He checked how high the mercury was and then shook it down just to be sure.

"This lady was shopping at the market on Centre Street," Tim told him.

"John Carter's place," Bill Cornreid, the other driver, added.

Tim nodded. "That's the one. Anyway, John said she was shopping there a bit ago. Then she stopped dead and fell over. John said that she had been perspiring and complaining about it being hot right before she collapsed."

Alan nodded as he stared at the woman. "Thank you, gentlemen. Can you send in a nurse on your way back to your ambulance?"

"Sure, Doctor," Bill said.

The blond-haired driver gave the woman a reassuring smile, and then he headed for the door with his partner. Alan turned his attention to his patient. Her face was flushed and she perspired profusely. Sweat matted the edges of her hair. She looked more worried than sick, though.

"I'm Dr. Keener. Now the first thing I need to know is what your

6

name is."

"I'm Sarah Jenkins, Doctor, and I need to get home."

Alan squeezed her wrist to check her pulse. It was fast, but that could be because she was worried and anxious.

"That's a good idea. I need you to get home. It doesn't look good on my record if I can't cure my patients." He smiled at her. "But before I can send you home, I'm going to try and figure out why a lady like you took such an undignified fall in the market. Now, if you will open your mouth, I will take your temperature. Let's get an idea why you're sweating in a cool room."

Sarah arched her eyebrows. "This room is cool?"

Alan nodded. "Now open up."

Sarah obeyed and Alan stuck the thermometer in her mouth.

Harriet Dinning, a nurse Alan worked with frequently, walked into the room. She was a young woman about Sarah's age. Alan hoped she would help ease his patient's fears.

After a minute, Alan removed the thermometer and looked at it. Sarah's temperature was one hundred and four degrees. With a fever that high, it was no wonder that she had fallen. The poor woman must feel miserable. Alan examined her head for contusions in case she'd given herself a concussion in the fall. Sarah didn't wince as if she had hurt herself. He didn't feel any lumps either. She's been lucky.

As Harriet bent over to wipe Sarah's forehead with a cool cloth, Sarah covered her mouth and coughed. It was a harsh cough, but it produced nothing. Harriet pulled back quickly.

Sarah covered her mouth. "I'm sorry."

Harriet just smiled. "That's all right. I've had worse on me."

"How long have you had that cough?" Alan asked.

Sarah shook her head. "Just now. This was the first time."

"And how about your fever?"

Sarah frowned. "I started feeling warm yesterday. It's nothing really. It might be the Indian summer," she admitted.

"What Indian summer? It's fifty degrees outside. Is your fever all that is bothering you?"

The young woman lowered her eyes and shook her head. "I've been feeling dizzy and achy all over for a couple days."

Alan nodded. He touched the sides of her neck with his hand. Her glands weren't swollen. That was a good sign. Her fainting worried him, though.

7

"Open your mouth, please," he asked.

Sarah did so. Alan moved the overhead lamp so that it shone down her throat. Then he held her tongue down with a wooden depressor. He saw no swelling, spots or discoloration that he could see.

Alan stepped back and tossed the depressor into the trashcan.

"Can you sit up on your own, Mrs. Jenkins?" he asked.

Sarah nodded and pushed herself up on her elbows and then swung her legs over the edge of the table. Her arms trembled as she put her weight on them.

"You need bed rest, Mrs. Jenkins, and lots of it," Alan told her.

Sarah snorted and rolled her eyes. "I have two sons, Doctor. A mother can never rest."

Alan could sympathize with her. He remembered being a young boy. He and Rudolf had run their mother ragged as they explored the forests and town streets around their home on the outskirts of Berlin. Alan also remembered the times when his mother had drawn so heavily from her hidden reserve of mother's energy that she had fallen victim to illnesses that usually wouldn't have stopped her.

Alan cocked his head to the side and told Sarah, "If a mother doesn't get the rest she needs, then a mother will spend a long time recovering from the flu."

Sarah frowned. "Can't you give me something for it? A pill or a powder? I can't be sick."

Alan shook his head. "Sadly, no. Modern medicine, for all its advantages, still does not fully understand the human body. In your case, we have learned in the past few years that germs cause the flu and even a cold. We know this, but we don't know a way to stop them."

"It sounds a lot like standing on the train tracks and watching the train come and hit you. You know it's coming, but you don't do anything about it." Sarah said.

Alan smiled and nodded. "Yes, it's something like that. However, it's not a matter of don't but can't."

"If you can't stop it, then why worry about it?"

"Because someone will stop it eventually. The more doctors and researchers can do now to make finding a cure easier, the faster that cure will be found. We doctors build on the discoveries of those doctors who came before us. It's kind of like a snowball rolling down a hill and getting bigger and bigger."

Sarah shook her head. "But I've still got to deal with this flu now, and me with two boys to raise. Their father is not even around to help out. So I can't slow down."

She didn't have to say where her husband was. Nowadays, it was assumed if a husband was missing, then he was fighting in the war in Europe. The field doctors there certainly had to deal with a lot worse than influenza and colds.

"I am sorry, Mrs. Jenkins. It should only last a day or two. Aspirin powder can help with the fever and aches, but things will still have to run their course. Don't you remember how it was this spring with the flu? It hit a lot of people and made their lives miserable for three days."

"I was lucky. It missed me then," Sarah said.

"Well, I guess it's your turn now," Alan said, smiling.

Alan hated being in this position. What good was being a doctor if he couldn't help people? He could only tell them they were sick in situations like this, and the patients already knew that. What they wanted was to be cured. So many cures seemed to be within the grasp of medicine and yet still just out of reach. Influenza was one of those things. Researchers knew what caused it, in theory, but they hadn't been able to stop it so far.

"That's not much of a reassurance," Sarah said. "I doubt I'll have much of a house left if I'm stuck in my bed for three days."

"I'm afraid that it's all I can give you. Do you have aspirin at home? If not, I can have the nurse fetch you some," Alan offered.

Sarah nodded. "I have some in the medicine chest in my bathroom."

"Good. I can call a taxi to take you home."

The young mother smiled weakly. "Please do. I certainly don't feel like walking home. Who knows where I would fall down? People might think I'm drunk."

Alan had Harriet escort Sarah to the front of the hospital to the Baltimore Avenue entrance. He went to the phone and called for a taxi.

He took his notes to his office to write up a summary for his files. He didn't think he would see Mrs. Jenkins again, but there always was a chance she might develop pneumonia as a complication of the flu, especially if she didn't get the rest she needed. In that instance, the notes would be helpful to know more about her condition and what little treatment she had received today.

Alan sat down in the wooden chair and noticed the copy of the *Cumberland Evening Times*. He picked it up to move it off to the side and one word caught his attention. Flu.

It wasn't the headline story. There could only be one headline story with the Great War winding down, but the story was on the front page. The Spanish Flu had reappeared and was spreading in Europe, which was unusual. It had been rampant earlier in the year when Alan had been readying himself for graduation from medical school. The Spanish Flu had spread through Europe rapidly, seemingly condensing all of the symptoms and problems associated with a normal flu into a few days. However, because it so virulent, it had seemed like it infected everyone at the same time. Then it had vanished over the summer. Now, apparently it was back and just as bad as it have been last spring.

He also noted the articles on the fighting in Europe with a twinge of guilt. It most definitely came because he wasn't fighting, but for which side he wasn't sure.

Alan Keener had been born Alex Krieger in Berlin, Germany. He was a naturalized citizen because he had fallen in love with the United States when he came here to attend medical school at Johns Hopkins in Baltimore. Then the war had broken out and his family had written him asking him to come home and fight for Kaiser Wilhelm as many good Germans were doing. He had put them off by saying he would be of more use to the Kaiser as a fully trained doctor. Then the United States had entered the war and the pleas from home became more urgent. Alex had a duty to his homeland his parents told him. He needed to be a good son and return home.

Alan had resisted, citing his studies and his desire to heal not kill. Then his brother Rudolf had been killed in an early battle and Alan had had to deal with the accusations of being a traitor from his parents.

"My only son has been killed by the Americans. May all who live there rot in Hell," his mother had written in her last letter to him.

And so, Alex Kreiger had become Alan Keener.

He couldn't become involved in the fighting against his people anyway. The truth was that the U.S. government wasn't anxious to have him fight in the war. They weren't entirely sure how loyal a newly naturalized citizen born in Germany was to his new country.

One reason Alan had changed his name from the German-sounding Alex to the solid American name Alan was that Alan had realized that as a German, he attracted suspicion. He'd taken a similar approach with his surname. That he been harder to part with, but it seemed to be in line with the fact that his parents had disowned him as a Kreiger. He had only formalized his parents' actions.

When his shift at the hospital was over, Alan walked to his small home on Columbia Street. The walk was enjoyable and some days when he was swamped by paperwork and stuck at his desk, it was the only exercise he got. Even in the dead of winter, Alan would walk at a quick clip so that he could raise sheen of sweat by the time he reached his home or the hospital.

His home was a brick house with a large front porch. Alan liked the fact that it was only a few blocks from the school. He took his coat off in the vestibule and hung it on a hook between the front doors. Then he walked through the interior door.

The sound of running feet greeted him. Three-year-old Anne threw herself at him. She was not quite three-feet of pure energy. Her brown hair was tied back in a ponytail that flew out behind her she ran. She was dressed in a pink dress with a flower stitched on the front.

"Papa! Papa!"

Alan laughed and scooped his daughter up and hugged her. She laughed and hugged him tightly around the neck.

Emily waddled into view. She looked like a larger version of Anne with her brown hair pulled back in a ponytail and wearing a loose-fitting pink maternity dress. She must not have gone out today if her hair was still just pulled back out of her face and not combed and braided. She looked tired. Alan supposed he would be too if he had to balance an extra fifty pounds on his stomach.

He walked over and kissed his wife on the cheek. He laid a hand on her belly and rubbed it, trying to elicit a response from the baby.

"How are you feeling?" he asked.

"Just fine, doctor," she said, smiling.

Emily was pregnant with their second child, who was due in two months. Alan secretly hoped it was a boy, but he kept his thoughts to himself. He wondered if Emily would have the same problem with having two children as Sarah Jenkins had said she had with her sons. Anne certainly was full of energy.

"Dinner is ready. You timed your return perfectly," Emily said.

"I just followed my nose all the way home," Alan said.

Anne laughed and squeezed his nose. He nuzzled her and snorted. She laughed again. It was a high-pitched squeal that was a pure delight to hear.

Alan walked with them back into the kitchen. He put Anne in her

11

seat and then sat down next to her while Emily served the chicken and rice.

"I don't like rice," Anne said.

"Why not?" Emily asked.

"It looks like bugs."

"Well, if they are bugs, your mother cooked them so they are all right to eat now," Alan told her.

"Okay," Anne agreed.

Emily lightly swatted Alan on the head with a wooden spoon.

"Owww!" he said, rubbing his head.

Alan said the prayer over the meal and then they began to eat. Emily could barely get near the table because her stomach was so swollen.

"How was work?" she asked.

"Quiet." Alan paused. "It looks like we're coming into the flu season. You need to watch out so you don't get sick. Your resistance is not as strong as it usually is since you're pregnant."

Emily nodded. "I realize that."

"How was your day?" Alan asked.

"Fine, I caught Anne burying apples — entire apples, mind you — in the backyard."

"Why did you do that, Anne?" Alan asked his daughter.

"I want to grow apple trees," she said innocently.

Alan laughed.

Emily arched her eyebrows. "I'm glad you find it funny. You can dig them up."

"Why me?"

"Because I'm not sure Anne found them all and I can't bend down to check," Emily said.

Alan rolled his eyes. "Can I at least wait until my day off?"

Emily shrugged. "As long as there aren't apple tree branches showing through the ground when you get around to it."

"At least then I would know where the apples are buried."

After dinner, Alan washed the dishes while Emily took Anne upstairs to get her ready for bed. When he finished drying the last of the dishes, he followed them upstairs.

Emily had given Anne a bath and read her. Then she said her prayers and Emily tucked her into bed. That's when Alan came in to kiss her goodnight.

He would remember it as his last happy day with his daughter.

Thursday,
September 26, 1918

Olivia Henderson paused on the porch of the red-brick house on Mechanic Street where her daughter's family lived. It was unusual to not hear the boys yelling and playing. Sometimes when they were outside playing with friends, she could hear their shouts and laughs a block away.

This morning, all she could hear was the clop-clop of a horse's hoofs as someone rode it down the brick-paved street.

Olivia wondered if Sarah and the boys had forgotten she was coming over this morning and they had gone somewhere else. But Sarah was the one who had asked her to come over and help out while she tried to get some rest and recover from the flu.

She opened the door and called, "Hello! Sarah? Gregory? Paul?"

Two little forms charged at her from the kitchen at the back of the house. Gregory and Paul hit her so hard they almost knocked Olivia back into the door. She staggered but remained standing.

She smiled at the enthusiastic greeting, but then she realized they hadn't said anything and they were both shaking. She could feel them trembling as they clutched at her waist.

She patted them on the head. "What's wrong, boys? Aren't you going to tell Grandmother hello?"

Gregory looked up. "Some…something bad happened, Grandmother."

Paul burst out crying.

Olivia pried their arms from around her. Then she took them by the hands and walked into the front parlor. She sat the boys down on the sofa and then sat down in the nearby rocking chair.

It was unusual to see her grandsons so scared. Whatever trouble they had gotten themselves into must have been pretty bad to have them so scared. She wondered if they had broken Sarah's good china. It had taken her years to buy all the pieces, a piece at a time. With the

13

way the boys played and ran, one of them could have easily fallen into the china cabinet sent all of the dishes to the floor.

"Did you boys break something?" Olivia asked.

Gregory shook his head. Paul lay on his side still crying.

"Then what is wrong? And where is your mother?"

"Something's wrong with her," Gregory whispered.

Olivia sat back in the rocking chair. "Oh, is that all. Yes, something is wrong with your mother. She's sick right now. That's why I came over. She needs to rest."

Gregory shook his head furiously. "No, something bad happened. We know she's sick. We took her a glass of orange juice this morning and she didn't move. She just looked scared...and there was blood."

The rocker snapped forward.

"Blood?" Olivia repeated.

Gregory nodded. "We were scared and ran out of the bedroom. Is Mama going to be all right? She hasn't said anything all morning."

Blood? Olivia stood up. What could be wrong with Sarah that caused her to bleed enough that boys would notice?

"You two stay here. I'm going to check on your mother."

Olivia climbed the oak stairs to the second floor. The master bedroom was at the front of the house at the end of the hallway. As she reached the top of the stairs, Olivia could see the door to the bedroom was ajar. The boys must have left it open.

"Sarah, it's Mother," Olivia called as she walked down the hallway. "You've got to wake up now. You've got the boys scared."

Olivia got to the doorway of the bedroom and looked inside.

Her scream made Gregory and Paul start to cry again.

Thursday afternoon was quiet at the hospital, which was typical. Despite Cumberland's size, most doctors tended to treat their patients in their homes. Patients only came to the hospital in instances of absolute emergency, scheduled surgeries, or if no one was at home to care for them.

Alan only had one emergency case to attend to so far; a house painter had fallen off a ladder and broken his arm. Alan set the arm, splinted it and wrapped it in plaster and gauze.

Other than that, he made rounds and kept a check on the patients in the wards. Eight patients filled the wards and two of the private rooms so it didn't take long. The nurses had made them comfortable and so there was little for Alan to do.

Western Maryland hospital had originally been built in 1892 with room for twenty-three patients. An addition of four wards, twenty-one rooms, a dining room and three bathrooms was added in 1910. A hydraulic elevator had also been added at that time. Four years later, two operating rooms, a sterilizing room, more wards and patient rooms were added. Although not new, Western Maryland was a modern hospital.

Alan wondered when he would be able to set out on his own and establish his own practice. He longed to do research again as he had at Johns Hopkins. Sometimes, when he was extremely bored, he went to the hospital's lab and tinkered with the equipment.

Not today, though.

He sat down at his desk to read the *Cumberland Evening Times*. It had been delivered about an hour ago. First, he flipped through the pages to see if anything important caught his attention. It was a ritual he had started in medical school. With his free time so limited, he made sure he read the articles he most wanted to read first. Then if there were time, he would read other items in the newspaper that hadn't caught his attention the first time through.

What stopped him in Thursday's paper was the obituary for Sarah Jenkins. He didn't even skim the paper any further. The sight of her name in the obituaries so soon after Alan had seen her as a patient stopped him in his tracks. He read the notice quickly and then re-read it. Sarah's mother had found her dead this morning.

Alan dropped the paper.

It had just been the flu! A simple case of the flu! How could she have died so quickly?

The cause of death had been listed as pneumonia, but that was a typical complication of influenza.

He propped his drooping head up with his hands and slowly ran his hands through his light brown hair. It was impossible! Just impossible! She hadn't been that sick!

Sarah Jenkins had died less than a day after Alan had seen her. Less than day! How could her health have changed so quickly? She hadn't been in any danger yesterday morning. It had just been a simple case of the flu. It should have run its course in two or three days.

The first wave of the Spanish Flu had begun last February during his final semester in medical school. The flu had first appeared in San Sebastian, Spain, which led to the name of the flu. Those who contracted the flu had burned with fever and felt achy, but they rested for three days and recovered. It had spread quickly, but it hadn't been deadly.

In March, more than a thousand Ford automobile factory workers had called in sick with Spanish Flu. More than one-quarter of San Quentin's nineteen hundred prisoners had become sick in April and May with the flu. They lived. It had been uncomfortable and inconvenient not deadly.

The flu had even caused problems to the war effort on both sides of the battlefield. King George V of England's naval fleet couldn't put to sea for three days because more than ten thousand sailors were sick. German General Erich von Ludendorff said that the flu contributed to the defeat of his July offensive because he couldn't field enough soldiers.

Then the flu had disappeared for most of the summer only to reappear in America late last month. On August 28, eight sailors at Boston's Commonwealth Pier fell sick with the flu. The next day, fifty-eight sailors were sick. Two days later, one hundred and nineteen sailors were sick and the first civilian was admitted to Boston City Hospital. At the end of the first week of September, twelve days after the first appearance of the second wave of flu, three people had died. Also on that day, the flu first appeared at an army fort thirty miles west of Boston.

Spanish Influenza had hit Philadelphia about two weeks ago and then Fort Meade, between Baltimore and Washington D.C., a few days after that.

Just today, Alan had heard that about fifty thousand people in Massachusetts had Spanish Flu and more than one hundred and fifty had died in Boston alone. Thousands of people had already died from the second wave of this deadly form of flu. It might have the same name, but it was definitely a deadlier flu.

Was it really so different from the typical annual influenza outbreaks?

Had the Spanish Flu killed its first victim in Allegany County?

Alan stood up and walked into the hallway. He looked around and then walked two doors down to Dr. Ralph Hyatt's office. Dr. Hyatt was the chief doctor for the Western Maryland Hospital.

The door was open, but Alan knocked on the doorframe. Dr. Hyatt wasn't the sort of man you walked in on without an invitation. The older man looked up from a report he was writing. He was completely bald except for a few tufts of white hair around his ears. His eyebrows were bushy white. His skin sagged around his cheeks and neck.

Dr. Hyatt looked over the top of his reading glasses to stare at Alan.

"Come in, Doctor." His voice had a certain elegance to it that reassured Dr. Hyatt's patients even when the doctor delivered bad news to them.

Alan walked in and stood in front of the wide oak desk. Dr. Hyatt placed his pen in the holder and took his reading glasses off.

"What brings you in, Dr. Keener?"

"This, Dr. Hyatt."

Alan set the newspaper on Hyatt's desk and pointed to the obituary. Hyatt read the notice quickly and looked up.

"You'll have to explain what it is that you want me to see. I don't believe I knew this young woman," Hyatt said.

"Sarah Jenkins was alive yesterday. She was in here for treatment."

"And you were the doctor in attendance?"

Alan nodded.

The bushy eyebrows raised a fraction of an inch. "So if she was so ill, why did you send her home? Pneumonia certainly warrants admittance to the hospital. We could have taken care of her here and given her the medical attention she obviously needed."

"She didn't *obviously* need medical attention yesterday. She wasn't that ill," Alan insisted.

"This notice says that she died of pneumonia. That doesn't happen overnight, especially a case that is severe enough to kill someone. She must have been showing signs when she was in here."

Alan shook his head. "She had a fever, which caused her to perspire. Her pulse was slightly elevated and she had a cough. There was nothing to indicate that it was anything more than influenza and a mild case of that."

Hyatt tapped nervously on the newspaper.

"And you believe that it was something else?" Hyatt asked.

Alan frowned. "It was influenza. Spanish Influenza. Nothing else could have developed so quickly."

Hyatt shook his head. "Spanish Influenza isn't that deadly."

"I'm not talking about what went around last spring. I'm talking about the new variation that has been spreading this past month," Alan said.

"There haven't been any cases around here."

Hyatt liked to pride himself on the relative healthiness of the community without crediting the fact that Cumberland just wasn't as densely packed as New York or Philadelphia, which helped slow the spread of any disease.

"Spanish Flu has spread from Boston to New York to Philadelphia in a month. We are certainly along that path, and that path is strewn with hundreds of dead people and thousands of ill ones. You know how fast the flu spread last spring. You didn't get it here at first then, but eventually it did hit here. That hasn't changed."

Just talking about the devastation of this flu scared Alan. He had still been in his last semester in medical school during the last outbreak. He had seen half of his class disappear as they took to their beds with fevers and pains. And all the while, the rest of the class had been looking at the cause through their microscopes.

They had seen the enemy in a way few people did. They could identify it, but they couldn't stop it. Combating a normal flu outbreak was impossible. How could he fight something that he couldn't see without a microscope? Treating it was like trying to paint the Mona Lisa with a house painter's brush.

"Baltimore is more likely to be hit than Cumberland," Hyatt said.

Baltimore was the state's largest city. Cumberland the second largest. If the first were to fall, wouldn't it make sense that the second should as well?

"Baltimore has been hit. And don't we receive passengers and workers daily off the railroad from Baltimore? If it hits Baltimore — and it already has, — it will hit here, which I believe it has done through Sarah Jenkins. We've got to alert the Board of Health to take precautions."

Hyatt waved a finger at Alan. "Watch your tone, Doctor. I have been practicing medicine for longer than you have been alive. You have been out of medical school less than a year. What makes you believe that your opinion is more learned than mine?"

"Dr. Hyatt, I have been trained from the beginning of my studies about germ theory. That is the basis of the influenza contagion. I'm sure you have lots of experience with influenza, but we're talking about a strain of influenza that has only been around for less than a year. My class studied it in medical school. I was doing research on the Spanish Flu when I graduated."

"Yes, and the research that you and others did showed there was no

Pfeiffer's Bacillus present. Spanish Influenza might not even be a strain of flu," Hyatt said.

In 1892, Dr. Friedrich Johann Pfeiffer was head of the research department at Berlin's Institute for Infectious Diseases. That year, he announced he had isolated a bacterium of people who had become ill with the 1890 flu. It was his contention that the bacterium researchers now called Pfeiffer's Bacillus was responsible for influenza.

The bacillus was a slender, rod-shaped bacterium that turned influenza deadly. Alan had always marveled that something so small, so microscopic, could cause so much devastation. Medicine was fast becoming a study of microscopic reactions rather than macroscopic treatments.

Alan shook his head. "Just a few days ago it was reported that researchers in Philadelphia have found the bacillus."

"Then perhaps this is not Spanish Influenza."

"Or maybe Pfeiffer was wrong. After all, there hasn't been a major epidemic since his discovery that we could test his theory against."

Hyatt rolled his eyes. "There you go questioning those with more experience than you. Not only me and Dr. Pfeiffer, but you cast aspersions against the entire medical profession. It is they who said that the bacillus was the indicator for influenza."

This was not going at all how Alan had hoped that it would. He had wanted Dr. Hyatt to recognize the threat and take action.

"It's not me who first raised the questions about Pfeiffer's Bacillus. It was the opinion of the researchers who have been studying this influenza and trying to contain it. The point is that Spanish Influenza, whether influenza or not, is something we are not used to dealing with," Alan said.

Hyatt leaned back in his chair and shook his head. "But you are assuming Mrs. Jenkins died of Spanish Influenza. Maybe it was something else; something you missed." He stabbed a finger in Alan's direction.

The accusation shook Alan. He had never been accused of incompetence before, but he knew Sarah Jenkins had not had pneumonia yesterday.

"I'm sure that's what people in Boston, New York and Philadelphia thought. Do you want to take the chance that this is my mistake when you can read the newspaper and see that people are dying?" Alan said in his defense.

Hyatt sighed. "Doctor, suppose for a moment that this is the first case of Spanish Influenza in Allegany County. What can we do to prevent its spread? And I say that with great reluctance. Medical science didn't cure Spanish Influenza last spring when it wasn't deadly. It went away on its own. If this is the first case as you propose, then we may have to allow it to run its course."

Alan sighed and shook his head. "This isn't like last spring. If we try to allow it to run its course, people will die. Maybe a lot of them. Can you just sit back and do nothing?"

Hyatt tossed his glasses across the desk in frustration. "Of course not, but what would you have us do? Have the doctors who have been dealing with this outbreak of influenza made any headway? Did your great researchers in medical school unravel the mysteries of the flu last spring?"

"No," Alan admitted.

"Then what can we do?"

"Watch for another case and draw blood and mucus samples to work on a vaccine. Other researchers are coming up with new theories everyday. We can try those. We need to find out who Mrs. Jenkins has had contact with over the last week and examine them for signs of influenza. If we can't cure it, then maybe we can isolate it and keep it from most of the population," Alan suggested.

Hyatt shook his head. "Neither is our job. We treat the ill. We don't do research or the job of the Board of Health."

Alan bounced to his feet. "Then we need to contact those that do those jobs. We should alert the Board of Health to the possibility and let them take the necessary actions to isolate the problem."

Hyatt folded the newspaper closed. "Let me be quite frank here, Dr. Keener. You are the problem here, not the flu. One case, if indeed it was a case and not simply a misdiagnosis on your part, is not a cause for alarm. If you announce to the public that we have a Spanish Influenza epidemic, it will cause a panic. When you have been a doctor for as long as I have been, you will realize this."

Alan straightened up. He tilted his head back and stared at the plaster ceiling for a few moments. He might as well have been talking to it for all the good it did to talk to Dr. Hyatt. The chief doctor only dealt with the illness he could see not that which might be coming. He was focused on his role as a hospital administrator who treats the sick and not on his role as a doctor who keeps people healthy.

Alan jammed his hands into his pocket. As he did, he felt his badge for the Volunteer Medical Service Corps. It was a small shield made of oxidized silver and showing the caduceus surmounted by the letters VMSC. He wondered if being a member could help him in this situation. Technically, he was a member of a back-up organization to the U.S. Public Health Service. Shouldn't that put him on equal footing with the Cumberland Board of Health in determining whether there was a crisis?

He started to pull it out of his pocket to show Dr. Hyatt, but then he stopped. Every doctor of draft age had joined the corps to avoid being called a slacker since many doctors were deferred in the draft because they had "essential jobs" among civilians. The shield was more to protect doctors from being labeled a coward or someone who wasn't doing his part in this war than it had to do with health. Alan's entire graduating class from medical school had paid their dollar and joined the Volunteer Medical Service Corps on graduation day.

Not for the first time, Alan wished that the Great War was over. If so, many of the doctors who had been drafted into the armed forces would return home. When they came home, they would be doctors who weren't so set in their ways by practicing years of standard medicine. The doctors who returned from the war will have been exposed to all types of death, injury and illness. They will have learned to think creatively and quickly about solutions.

Though that future was closer, those doctors would have to make it through the present for that to happen.

"Thank you for your time, Dr. Hyatt," Alan said.

The older doctor nodded. He lifted a file from the side of his desk, laid it in front of him and opened it. Then he reached across his desk and retrieved his glasses.

Alan left the office and walked down the hall to the telephone box mounted on the wall. He picked it up and asked the operator to connect him to the Jenkins's home. A man answered.

"Mr. Jenkins?" Alan asked, and then he remembered Sarah's husband was a soldier.

"No, I'm Carl Henderson. Sarah was my daughter."

"I'm Dr. Keener, sir. I practice at the Western Maryland Hospital. I was sorry to hear about your daughter, sir. Are your grandsons all right?" Alan asked.

"They're upset, of course. Despite what the newspaper said, they

21

are the ones who found their mother when she didn't wake up this morning. Thank heavens their grandmother came by to help clean the house and feed the boys."

What a dreadful final memory to have of their mother! Alan's mother was still alive. His final memory was of her hugging him as he went off to America not as she must have looked when she read his letter that said he would not be returning home to fight for Kaiser Wilhelm.

"Did the medical examiner ask for an autopsy?" Alan asked.

"Yes, he did. He said that he would perform it at the funeral parlor before they…before they…" Henderson choked back a sob.

"I understand what you mean, sir. You don't have to finish," Alan said. "Who is handling the arrangements?"

"John Wolford."

"How is your family doing?"

Alan wondered if other members of Sarah Jenkins's family were showing signs of the flu. They would be the most likely ones to be infected.

"How do you expect us to be doing at a time like this?" Henderson said, somewhat sharply.

"I'm not speaking emotionally, sir. How is your family doing health wise?"

Henderson paused. "Do you think we might have what Sarah had?"

Alan was surprised that the man had picked up so quickly on the direction of Alan's questions. Alan was a poor liar.

"I don't know. I just want to make sure that your family doesn't have to deal with any more tragedy," Alan explained.

"You didn't see my daughter. She was a beautiful girl, but I don't want to remember her like the way she looked this morning."

"Sarah complained yesterday about feeling achy and feverish. Does anyone else in your family show those symptoms?" Alan asked.

"We all seem to be fine," Henderson said slowly, cautiously.

Alan hesitated. The man needed reassurance that Alan couldn't give him.

"That's good. It's one less thing for you to worry about. If you see any signs of the flu among your family, get them to the hospital. Don't try and treat it yourself," Alan cautioned him.

"We will," said Henderson, his voice shaky.

Alan hung up the phone. He told Harriet Dinning, who was on duty at the admitting desk, that he was going to the funeral parlor the newspaper had listed for Sarah Jenkins's funeral.

"Are you going to see that poor woman?" Harriet asked.

"You mean Sarah Jenkins?"

Harriet nodded. "I feel so sorry for her children."

"It wasn't my fault," Alan snapped.

"I didn't say it was, Doctor."

Alan closed his eyes and nodded. "No, you didn't. I just overreacted. I'm sorry."

The Wolford Funeral Home was in downtown Cumberland on Centre Street. Alan walked down Decatur Street to Baltimore Street. He crossed the B&O Railroad tracks and continued down Baltimore Street until he reached St. Paul's Lutheran Church. Then he turned left onto South Centre Street.

The funeral home was a stone and wooden home that looked like a grand estate. Instead, it was a funeral home on a small lot in the city. Alan walked inside the building. He could see down the hallway and there was no one around. He walked down the hall and looked into the empty viewing parlors.

"Hello?" he called.

He heard some movement on the stairs. Then John Wolford appeared at the head of the stairs leading to the second floor. He was wearing a linen surgical gown to cover his suit.

"I thought I heard someone down there. What can I do for you, sir?" Wolford asked.

Alan had been in town long enough to make everyone's acquaintance, but truthfully, he hoped the undertaker was not someone he got to know well.

"I'm Dr. Keener from Western Maryland Hospital. I was told that the medical examiner was going to autopsy Sarah Jenkins here."

Wolford nodded and shook Alan's hand. "Hello, Doctor. Yes, Dr. McCullough is up here now. He's just getting ready to get started. Would you like to join us?"

Alan climbed the stairs and followed the mortician into the embalming room. They walked into a white-walled open room that was brightly lit. Makeup and embalming fluid shared the shelves on the wall with various saws, knives and needles. In the center of the room was a porcelain table where Sarah's body lay with a sheet pulled up to her neck.

Her eyes had a sunken look, but her lips looked brighter than usual. Alan nearly shuddered. Her cream-smooth skin was now marred with mahogany spots. It was hard to imagine that this woman had been healthy and happy just two days ago.

Jack McCullough stood on the other side of the table. He wore a white gown to protect his suit from blood and other material. His hands were inside rubber gloves and a gauze mask covered his face. He wore them in case the bodies he dealt with were infectious.

He opened his bag and lay out his tools on a table next to the embalming table.

Jack was fifty years old and steel-gray hair just a half inch long all over his head. He wore glasses with small, round lenses that made his face look very large. He also wore his perpetually sad expression. Alan liked the man because he had welcomed the Keeners without reservation to Cumberland.

"Why so sad?" Alan asked.

"Look at this woman, Alan. She shouldn't be dead and yet she is. This only reinforces to me once again that death cannot be conquered, at least not by mere man. Sometimes the reminders almost bring me to tears," Jack said quietly.

Alan hesitated, somewhat shaken by Jack's little speech. "I wanted to watch the autopsy and see what you find."

"Did you know this woman?" Jack asked.

"Not really. I only saw her for the first time yesterday."

Jack's gray eyebrows nudged up. "Was she sick then?"

Alan shook his head. "She had a fever and was achy. She also had the beginnings of a cough. That was all. Really. It was nothing out of the ordinary," he said more defensively than he meant.

Jack glanced at the body on the table. "Obviously it wasn't simply the beginning. You suspect something more, don't you?"

Alan stared at the body. What he suspected was dangerous. It could cause a panic, but one woman was dead. How many more needed to die before he would voice his suspicion?

Alan took a deep breath and said, "Spanish Influenza."

John Wolford gasped and grabbed for a gauze mask to protect himself. That wasn't as bad as Alan thought would happen. He had half expected John and Jack to run out of the room.

Jack's eyes widened slightly. "That's a nasty bit of business, that is. I would hate to be in Boston right now."

"Or maybe Cumberland," Alan added. "Can you tell if that's what she had?"

Jack shrugged. "You could probably do a better job at it than me. I don't have research equipment in my office. I can give you a sample from her lungs and you can examine it for Pfeiffer's Bacillus. Given how quickly she died, I would say if she appeared to have the flu, she most likely did. Very little else could have done this so quickly."

"If that's the case, then we need to know how it's being transmitted and what makes it deadly. What is different between now and what we dealt with last spring?"

"Well then, maybe we can find out what made it so deadly to Mrs. Jenkins," Jack said.

He pulled back the sheet covering Sarah to begin the autopsy. Alan felt a twinge of embarrassment staring at the body of the young, nude woman. Wolford served as a secretary, writing down the things that Jack told him so that the medical examiner would be able to write up his report later.

Besides the mahogany spots on her face, much of Sarah Jenkins's feet had changed color.

"Her feet are black," Alan noted.

Jack looked from Sarah's head to her feet. They were dark. Jack rubbed at them.

"It isn't anything on the exterior of her skin and there's no swelling. I would say the tissue is dead," Jack offered.

"What could have caused that? Flu doesn't attack the feet," Alan said.

"I'm not sure at the moment."

Jack used a scalpel to cut open the dead woman's flesh. It parted easily under the sharp blade. He cut a Y-shaped incision from her belly to her neck. Then he used a bone saw to cut through the woman's sternum. He pulled open the rib cage, cracking the ribs.

Alan winced and looked away. He had never been able to depersonalize a patient the way a medical examiner or mortician could.

"Ah," Jack said.

Alan's head snapped around. "What? You already know what happened?"

Jack nodded. "She drowned."

"Drowned? She was nowhere near water. She was found in her bedroom."

"Nevertheless, she drowned even if it was inside her home. Drowning is a condition where you suffocate because there is fluid in your

25

lungs and not air." He tapped Sarah's lungs with a wooden probe. "That's exactly what happened here."

Alan stared at her lungs. They were red and engorged, not the white lumps of tissue he had expected. They had not deflated when Sarah had stopped breathing.

Jack picked up a scalpel and made a small incision in the lungs. As soon as he did, reddish fluid began to seep out of the lung. He dipped his gloved finger into the fluid and raised it closer to his glasses so he could stare closely at it.

"There's blood mixed in with the fluid. That gives it the color," Jack said.

"Her breathing was clear yesterday afternoon," Alan said.

Then he remembered how she had coughed. Maybe her lungs hadn't been so clear. But he hadn't heard anything through the stethoscope. Had he missed something?

"My opinion is that she died of acute pneumonia. It's pretty obvious," pronounced Jack.

"It wasn't yesterday," he said defensively. "She only had the flu."

Jack rolled his eyes. "Stop acting defensive, Alan. I'm not accusing you. I'm just explaining what happened to her. It's what you wanted me to do, isn't it?"

Alan nodded numbly.

"Her body tried to fight off the flu in her lungs, but it reacted too strongly to the disease and wound up doing more harm than good," Jack said.

"Then the flu didn't kill her."

"Not directly. I already said death was from pneumonia, but that is splitting hairs."

Alan had seen this woman yesterday and she had been relatively healthy. At that point, he had had the opportunity to help her, but he had missed something and allowed her to go home…to go home and die. He had missed something that was so deadly that it had killed her less than a day later.

How could he have overlooked something like that? What were the signs that he hadn't seen? Was he really as inexperienced as Dr. Hyatt had said? Would Hyatt or one of the other senior doctors have found something that Alan had missed?

"Can I get some tissue samples?" Alan asked.

Alan knew a pathologist on staff at the hospital who could examine the tissue samples and maybe give him a clue of what had happened. Sarah Jenkins might have died of pneumonia, but something created the situation, something had compromised Sarah's natural defenses enough, to allow the pneumonia free reign in her body.

"Of what?" Jack asked.

"Her lungs. I want to see if there's any influenza left in her lungs." Alan paused. "You'd better add some tissue from her feet, as well."

He wasn't going to chance missing anything this time.

Alan needed to know. He needed to know what he had missed and why he had missed it. He couldn't let this happen again to some other innocent person that trusted him. He wasn't intending to see if the Spanish Flu bypassed Allegany County or not like Dr. Hyatt would do. Alan was going to do whatever it took to find a way to keep this from happening from anyone else.

FRIDAY, SEPTEMBER 27, 1918

John Carter could hear the medicine show huckster outside the market calling out to everyone within earshot about his "elixir of health" made from "a formula developed by the Father of Medicine." John had been listening to the spiel for an hour now. It was enough to make him sick and he doubted that the elixir of health would make him feel any better.

The building lot next to the Centre Street Market was empty since the home on it had burned down two years ago in a blaze that had had John on his knees thanking the dear Lord that the market had brick walls and a slate roof that resisted catching fire. Even so, his family had spent that night throwing buckets of water on three sides of the market to keep it wet and less likely to catch fire. The debris from the fire had been cleared away a few weeks after the fire and the lot leveled in the hopes of preparing it for a new home. It had sat vacant since then.

John's son, Frank, had considered buying the lot as a place to leave wagons, horses and automobiles as their owners shopped in the market or maybe even expanding the store to add more aisles and more products. Frank was always thinking ahead like that, trying to find ways to improve the market. John knew that the market he started would flourish under Frank's guidance as soon as Frank came home from the war.

If he came home.

John scolded himself for thinking like that. He closed his eyes and offered up a quick prayer, asking God to watch over Frank and bring him home safely.

John should be spending his days fishing under the shade of an oak tree on the banks of North Branch, but now he had to care for his business until his son returned home. John didn't want to see the business he had started thirty years ago die because of the war. He wanted Frank

28

to have a chance to make all of his grand dreams for the market come true.

Right now, John regretted that Frank hadn't purchased the empty lot. If he had, John would be able to run this huckster off his property now. John shouldn't have to put up with this constant sales call. Let the man pitch his cure-all on Baltimore Street or Virginia Avenue. Hank Goodfellow, the owner of the lot, had been drafted so John couldn't even call him to complain about what was happening on his property. Hank would have shown the huckster the business end of his shotgun to run him off. John considered doing it himself. Then the huckster could see if this magnificent elixir of health could cure a pound a buck-shot where the sun doesn't shine.

John stopped stacking cans of potatoes on the shelves and wiped the sweat from his forehead. He hadn't realized he had been working so hard that he had worked up a sweat. He filled a glass at the sink at the back of the store and drank some cold water.

The huckster took a deep breath at the conclusion of his spiel and started up once more. John found himself hoping someone would buy a bottle of the elixir just so the man would shut up for longer than it took him to catch his breath. John couldn't take anymore of this.

He walked out the back door and over to the lot.

The huckster stood near the sidewalk in a well-worn gray suit that looked a bit too shiny at the elbows and seat. He had a small folding ta-ble set up in front of him and called out to anyone who happened nearby. Sometimes he even called out to cars as they drove by his location.

"Are you feeling under the weather, Neighbor? Do you have a fe-ver? Aches? Arthritis? Dandruff? Or maybe you are just feeling a little sluggish? Dr. Riley's Patented Omni-Sol Health Elixir can help you. How do I know? I am Dr. Riley and I have studied the philosophies of health from the masters. I have learned that most medicines only treat the symptoms and not the causes of an illness. Dr. Riley's Patented Omni-Sol Health Elixir is designed using the ancient philosophies and formulas of the Father of Medicine. The ingredients in Dr. Riley's Pa-tented Omni-Sol Health Elixir regulate and align the body's systems to allow the body itself to fight off illness and disease."

John could see other signs that the huckster had seen better days. Rather than presenting a show filled with singers and comedians, this man worked alone. That was probably the reason no one was paying attention to the man. He was all pitch and no fun. There was nothing for an audience to enjoy and no reason for them to stop and listen to the huckster. He gave them no honey to take with his bitter-pill pitch.

John walked up behind the man. "Why don't you join the army?" he said.

The man stopped his routine and turned to look at John. A too-wide smile was plastered on his face. Perhaps the man thought that he could coerce John into buying.

"Ah, a patriot. I salute you, sir," the man said.

The huckster's hand flicked up to his forehead in a poor salute. John wanted to knock down the mocking gesture.

"You should be saluting an officer not a grocer."

"But I have. I am a veteran of the Spanish American War. I fought with former President Teddy Roosevelt and rode beside him on his famous charge up San Juan Hill."

John rolled his eyes. "Maybe if they gave you a pop gun. Those spectacles you're wearing don't fool me none. You're no more than thirty years old."

Dr. Riley grinned. He puffed out his chest and tapped on it. "I just appear that way because Dr. Riley's Patented Omni-Sol Health Elixir has helped me maintain my robust health."

"Then why aren't you fighting now? Why are you bothering hard-working people?"

"I'm glad that you asked that, sir."

John groaned. Everything he said was going to lead to the pitch for the cure-all. Maybe he should buy a bottle. Then he could use the bottle to conk this fool on the head.

"My calling has led me to deal in health not death. I can do more good by making sure those who remain at the home front are able to continue the machinations of our grand society that our soldiers are fighting for in the forests and cities of Europe. I do this sacred duty with the aid of Dr. Riley's Patented Omni-Sol Health Elixir," the huckster said.

John snorted.

"Perhaps you would care for a bottle of the elixir? You look a bit peaked. For just one dollar, this bottle will restore your health in a matter of hours. Its medicinal properties are world-renowned. Within a day, you will feel years younger. As you said yourself, I, a veteran of the Spanish American War, look no older than thirty years. What greater testimony of the effectiveness of Dr. Riley's Patented Omni-Sol

Health Elixir could you have than your own words?"

John knew his "testimony" was more the huckster's words than his but what use would it be to argue the point? John wanted quiet and arguing wouldn't get him that.

"What would make me feel better is for you to be quiet," John said firmly.

"If I was quiet, how would I be able to share the secret of health with the good people of Cumberland?" the huckster said. He held up his arms and turned in a small circle.

"If you aren't quiet, then I will have to call the police and have you arrested for disturbing the peace," John snapped, harsher than he had meant to but his head was hurting and this man's voice only made John's pain increase.

John wiped his forehead with his handkerchief. It was very warm for fall day. He might have to turn on the ceiling fans in the store. It appeared as if an Indian summer might be starting.

Dr. Riley frowned and nodded. "There is no need for the police. I am sorry to have annoyed you, sir. I was under the impression that the residents of the Queen City were friendly. It seems I have found one who is not. I'll be moving along."

John glared at him. "You do that."

He turned and walked back to the store, looking forward to some peace and quiet. Maybe he would take some headache powder to rid himself of the headache that had started.

Alan Keener looked over Dr. Peter Markwood's shoulder. The gray-haired doctor was the pathologist at the Western Maryland Hospital. He was bent over a microscope studying the lung tissue samples that Alan had removed from Sarah Jenkins's body.

The room was large enough for two people to work in, though Peter was usually the only person in here. A workbench lined two walls. It was covered with gas burners, glassware, two microscopes and an autoclave. It was perpetually humid in the room because of the steam coming out of the autoclave. Peter generally left the window cracked to try and keep the room at a decent temperature.

Peter shrugged to push Alan back away from him.

"Give me some room, boy, or we're both going to fall over this table," Peter said. His voice was deep and rough like sandpaper.

Alan stepped back and began to pace the width of the laboratory.

"You've been studying those samples since yesterday, Peter. Haven't you found anything yet?"

"I've found plenty. I'm just trying to make sense of what it means."

The older doctor straightened up from the microscope and rubbed his eyes. He pulled a handkerchief from his pocked and wiped the sweat from his forehead.

"So what have you found so far? Maybe I can help you figure it out," Alan suggested.

Alan wanted answers and he wasn't getting any.

Peter yawned and then nodded. "The tissue from the young woman's feet is easiest to understand. Jack was right. It is dead tissue."

"Of course it's dead. She was dead, Peter."

"Her feet died prior to the rest of her body. She hadn't gotten any blood into her feet for a while before she actually died or if she was getting blood down there, it wasn't oxygenated blood. That's what I think is the most-likely answer judging by some of my other findings. Her feet went cyanotic and the tissue died. Her hands would have been next. It would also explain the spots you said that you saw on her face as well. The spots are dead tissue as well."

"And that's because her lungs were so filled with fluid that she hadn't been able to breathe. Jack McCullough said she drowned," Alan said.

Peter nodded. "More than that. A good amount of the fluid in her lungs was blood. The alveoli and capillaries in her lungs had burst."

If the lungs were looked at as in upside down tree. The trachea would be the trunk and the primary bronchus would be two main limbs that split off the trunk. The bronchi and bronchioles would be smaller and smaller branches and the alveoli would be the leaves. If the alveoli had burst, the lungs would have lost their ability to drawn in oxygen properly.

Peter said, "Now the question is how that fluid got in there so quickly when you said she showed very little signs of congestion the day before she died."

"That's right. She had a mild case of the flu, if that," Alan said quickly.

Peter nodded. "Yes, she had the flu. I found the bacillus in the lung tissue. It took awhile to find it because there is a lot of other microscopic debris in the fluid. I had to filter it a few times."

Alan snapped his fingers. "I knew it."

"Don't look so happy, Alan. From what I've read, the spring cases of the Spanish Flu didn't have Pfeiffer's Bacillus. However, the fall cases, the deadly cases, do have the bacillus. Just like was reported in Philadelphia. Why the difference?"

Alan felt almost guilty for having his suspicions confirmed. He had been right, though, and the esteemed Dr. Hyatt had been wrong. The guilt came from knowing that it would have been a lot better for everyone if Dr. Hyatt had been right.

"I don't know why there's a difference. You're the pathologist, not me. Maybe the presence of Pfeiffer's Bacillus changes the flu from being something that makes you sick to something that kills you. Does it matter? We know it's Spanish Flu."

Peter rubbed his eyes and replaced his glasses on his face. "Yes, it matters. We're not theorizing research here. We're dealing with lives and if we make a mistake, it could kill just as many people as not. Remember, I mentioned the bacillus?" Alan nodded. "Well, it was theorized that doctors could identify the presence of influenza by the presence of Pfeiffer's Bacillus. We've acted for a generation believing that and yet, the Spanish Flu's first appearance came without that warning. There was no bacillus found last spring. Now either the researchers were wrong all those years ago, which may have cost lives in the interim or maybe the Spanish Flu isn't influenza, just as it isn't Spanish."

The flu had been named Spanish because it had first been reported in Spain, but it had truly been a worldwide epidemic last spring that hadn't remained long in Spain and had also seemed to spring up in other places at about the same time as it appeared in Spain just as it appeared to be doing now.

"I think we should at least wire some of the other cities and see what they might be doing that is working or at least helping," suggested Alan.

Peter nodded. "That would be a good precaution. It also wouldn't hurt to isolate any other suspected cases that come in. I can analyze throat swabs and search for the bacillus. If I find it, we'll deal with it. If not, we can send them home."

"Not that it will help much. This thing just spreads so fast by the time someone shows any signs of having the flu, he may already have infected a hundred people."

Peter rubbed his chin. "That is the problem, isn't it? It has spread down the eastern seaboard too fast. It can't be a chain reaction at least not the way we think of it."

"What about a vaccine? If we can inoculate people against Spanish Influenza early enough, we can halt its spread."

Science had come so far. Modern medicine could control or prevent cholera, typhoid and yellow fever. Some of those things had been deadlier and more complicated than the flu.

Peter snorted. "Don't you think there are people working on that now? The problem is you need to find someone who has immunity against the disease and compare that person's blood to everyone else. No one seems to have found such a person yet. Everyone seems to be catching it."

"Should we contact the Board of Health?"

Peter nodded and Alan nearly sighed with relief at having his concerns substantiated.

"Yes, they need to know the possibility of a Spanish Flu epidemic, but they won't be interested at this point. Not until we can show them that Mrs. Jenkins wasn't an isolated case."

"Is there truly an isolated case of influenza?" Alan asked.

Peter shrugged. "Probably not, but believing something and proving it are two different things. The Board of Health will want proof. And if we can give them proof, it's too late," Peter said.

"Too late?"

"By the time this is obviously a community health problem and the Board of Health takes an interest, we'll be in the same situation as Boston and Philadelphia."

The Spanish Flu was decimating Boston and Philadelphia. Thousands of people a day were catching it and hundreds a day were dying. The thought of the same thing happening in Cumberland made the small hairs on the back of Alan's neck stand on end.

Alan sent out the wires to the hospitals in Baltimore, Annapolis, Philadelphia, Washington, New York City, Albany, Newark and Boston later that afternoon. It was a simple message: "What are you doing that works to halt the spread of the Spanish Flu? What can we do to treat our patients who develop it?"

The first response came back right before Alan headed home for the day. It was from the Baltimore City Board of Health. It read: "Nothing can be done. Pray."

Saturday, September 28, 1918

Carson Riley stopped walking along Baltimore Street. He set his medicine case down and looked up at the Central YMCA. It occupied the top three floors above Rosenbaum's Shoes. He could use a pair of shoes, but his wallet was nearly empty.

He sighed and shook his head. He had once dreamed of being able to stay at a nice hotel like the one at the Queen City Station next to the B&O Railroad. He had never been able to move beyond the neat, but plain, YMCA. Not even during his best years when he actually had show performers did they stay in the best hotels.

Nowadays, he was lucky to be able to afford the YMCA. A bout of the flu back in April had laid Carson out for five days. He hadn't been able to pay Amanda Parson and Tyler McCutcheon, his singer and comic for his show, because he hadn't been able to sell any of Dr. Riley's Patented Omni-Sol Health Elixir. No one wanted to buy a cure-all from a sick man.

To this day, Carson still couldn't show his face in Annapolis where he had taken sick. The City by the Bay had been one of his best sales outlets. Politicians in the General Assembly were the biggest suckers for Dr. Riley's Patented Omni-Sol Health Elixir or maybe they just didn't want anyone to know they were drinking in the state house. With Carson's elixir, they could say they weren't drinking but were instead taking medicine. Carson was still trying to recover from the income loss and doing a poor job at that. No one bought medicine at the street shows anymore. Now the salesmen like him used newspaper advertisements that converted the glitz of a show into print.

Carson opened the door next to Rosenbaum's Shoes and started up the stairs. Halfway up, he stopped and perched his medicine case on the stairs.

His head throbbed so much that it felt like his brain was trying to push his eyes out from inside his head. He reached into the bag and pulled out a bottle of Dr. Riley's Patented Omni-Sol Health Elixir. He pulled the cork and drank a healthy gulp.

Then he reached into his pocket and lifted out a small tin of aspirin tablets. Carson knew what was in the Omni-Sol. While it might make someone feel better since it was eighty-proof alcohol, it couldn't do much to heal a person. Carson took two aspirin and swallowed them with another gulp of his health elixir.

"Ah, physician heal thyself," he murmured.

Maybe he would add some aspirin powder to his recipe so that his health elixir might actually have a health benefit and cure a headache. Maybe he could create the first alcoholic beverage that also cured the headache it created.

Carson put the bottle back into the bag and finished the walk up to the lobby. He stopped at the counter to check for any messages.

"Nothing today, Doctor," the young clerk said.

Carson smiled. The clerk was new at the YMCA. He hadn't realized yet that Carson's title was honorary, bestowed on Carson by himself. No one wanted to buy a cure-all from a non-doctor after all.

He trudged up the stairs to the fourth floor and let himself into the small room that looked out over the alley in the back of the building. He slid his bag under the bed and took his coat and tie off and tossed them onto the small stool.

The pitcher still had water in it from this morning. He poured some into the basin and splashed it on his face. He was feeling hot with a fever.

"Working too hard," he said to himself.

This was his third and final day in Cumberland. He had spent the days walking the streets and setting up his one-man presentation for Dr. Riley's Patented Omni-Sol Health Elixir. He missed the golden days when he had had a wonderful show with singers, musicians and women who danced while showing too much skin. Those had been in the days when it was easy to sell cure-alls, but there was too much competition from "legitimate" companies and too many stories of the uselessness of cure-alls put out by representatives of those companies. They were just non-medical people who hid behind the legitimacy of buildings with fancy names rather than walking among the people to learn their needs like Carson did.

He was not too high and mighty to walk the streets and find out what ailed the citizens of this great nation and then prescribe them Dr. Riley's Patented Omni-Sol Health Elixir. Only when he felt it would help ease the pains, of course.

What most people didn't realize was that Omni-Sol, which was based on the ancient philosophies of Hippocrates, treated the entire person. It cured the physical ailments, buoyed the spirit and eased the stress on the mind. That was the secret of health.

Carson smiled. Not even he believed his spiel.

He fell onto his bed and kicked off his shoes. His feet must have swollen to two sizes larger with all of the walking he had done today.

He laid back, closed his eyes and slept.

His eyes opened to darkness. The room felt like a steam bath. He lifted his hand to his face and realized it was slick with sweat.

He tried to lift his arms, but they felt so heavy he was more content to just lay on his bed. If only it wasn't so hot. It made it uncomfortable to stay in bed.

He could hear his blood pounding through his head. He imagined it as a wave crashing through his blood vessels. He wondered why the blood didn't surge out of his body.

"Carson."

Carson rolled his head to the side. Someone was standing in the dark corner of the room.

How had he gotten into the room? Carson had locked himself in his room.

"Who are you?" Carson asked.

Was he about to be robbed of the five dollars he had collected to-day?

The man stepped forward. His face and clothing changed every few seconds. He was every person that Carson had seen on the street today. The passerby who had threatened him. The woman who had bought a bottle of Omni-Sol. The police officer who had checked his license. On and on. When the faces had all flashed by once, they began again.

"Do you not recognize me?" the man said.

Carson was about to shake his head, but it felt so heavy that he didn't move.

"How can I? You keep changing," Carson mumbled.

"I am disappointed that you forget me so easily."

"Are you God?" Carson asked.

Carson's body shook. Could he actually be in the presence of God?

What would God want with him? He was just a no-account salesman.

The man smiled. "I am your god."

Carson's head throbbed and it was hard to breathe.

"Can you heal me?"

The man moved forward and touched Carson's forehead. The pain vanished.

"Thank you," Carson said.

"The time has come," the man said.

"What time? Please help me."

Carson sat back on his legs.

"The time has come. Man in his infinite arrogance feels that he has conquered death. With his medicines and vaccines, he feels that he can cheat death of its due reward. Yet, in the face of this, mankind battles each other condemning a generation to the death that it fears. It makes no sense.

"So the time has come for mankind to feel my wrath. Mankind must be reminded who is master and who is servant. Will you serve me, Carson?" the man asked.

How could Carson deny this man who had healed him? Who was he to be defiant to God?

"Yes, I will," Carson answered.

"You will be the instrument of my wrath. Mankind must be punished for destroying that which I have made. They must be punished for believing themselves to have conquered death. They must be brought back to me," his god commanded.

"Yes. I will be the instrument of your wrath."

The man smiled. He stepped back from the bed and turned from Carson.

"Wait!" Carson wanted to reach out to the man, but he couldn't lift his arm.

"You are my instrument. You have my power. It is the same power that I now show the earth."

The man continued to walk the few steps to the corner. He faded and mixed with the shadows in the corner of the room until he was gone.

Cow Lewis exhaled heavily and shook his head of dark brown hair. For a moment, he appeared more like a horse than his namesake.

Cow Lewis's real name was Calvin, but he stood six feet six inches tall and weighed two-hundred-and-eighty pounds. He didn't look like a Calvin. He looked like a Cow. People also tended to think that because Cow was so large that he was slow and slow thinking. He wasn't and many criminals in Cumberland had learned that when Cow beat them in a foot race to escape from custody or unraveled the motivation to a crime to catch the thief.

Because of his size and what people thought of him, Calvin had been dubbed Cow during his years at Allegany County High School on Greene Street.

Truth be told, his size had led him to become a police officer. He had no patience for farming and he was too intimidating as a shop-keeper. He might have worked at the Kelly-Springfield Company or Footer Dye Works, but he had no patience to work on an assembly line either.

So Cow had become a police officer and used his size to discourage bad behavior before it happened. He had found that he could walk into a bar brawl and things suddenly quieted down because no one, except for someone who was extremely drunk, wanted to chance Cow Lewis clapping him on the head. A blow like that was worse than a hangover the next day.

Cow considered himself a peacekeeper and he took the meaning of that title seriously.

He liked walking his beat along the streets of downtown Cumberland and talking to the residents he met, except for when he was break-ing in a new pair of shoes like today. Then he had blisters like the one he was nursing now. It was the size of a silver dollar. On days like this, he tried to do as little walking as possible and he was grumpy because of the constant pain he felt with each step. These were the days that people avoided him and only a fool committed a crime while he was on duty.

Jared Scell would find that out in a few minutes. Cow had been working quietly at his desk at police headquarters when Captain Loar had sent him to find Jared, a police officer who hadn't shown up for duty this morning.

Cow fumed. If he could walk his beat with blisters on his heels, then Jared could manage to show up for work. Cow would have a few words to share with Jared when he dragged him out of bed. It was bad enough that many of the police officers were considered slackers be-cause they weren't fighting in the Great War; Jared didn't have to live up to the label.

Cow walked up Vinegar Hill, wincing with each step. He found Jared's home on Maryland Avenue and stomped onto the porch. The wooden boards groaned with his weight. Cow shifted his weight to the balls of his feet to relieve a little bit of the pain from his blister.

Cow pounded on the door and rang the bell. No one answered. He didn't even hear anyone stirring inside the house.

He pounded again.

"Come on, Jared. It's Cow! Answer the door! Don't make me come in there and pull you down to headquarters in your nightshirt!" Cow yelled. He didn't care what Jared's neighbors might think of the noise he was making.

Still no answer.

Jared liked to visit the bars after work and had probably drunk too much list night. It would serve him right if he had to work with a hangover. If that were the case, Cow would make sure to do a lot of loud talking just to remind Jared how much pain he was making Cow endure.

Cow checked the door. It was unlocked. He stepped inside. The front parlor was empty.

"Jared! You had better be getting up, you slacker!"

Cow walked back to the dining room, which was also empty. Now what should he do? He walked up the stairs to the second floor.

"Come on, Jared. This is not making me any happier. It's way past time for you to be awake, you slacker!" Cow said.

He walked to the front bedroom and found Jared. Cow didn't even have to touch his fellow police officer to know that the young man was dead.

Jared Scell was sprawled diagonally across his bed with one arm hanging over the side pointing straight out. Cow moved up to the side of the bed and stared at Jared. The body was colored a brownish purple, particularly his face. His expression looked painful. A film of blood was on his mouth.

The huge officer suddenly gasped for breath. He realized that he had been holding his breath as he approached the bed. He backed away quickly. He stumbled against a rocking chair and nearly fell into it.

Cow spun around and hurried out of the room. He went downstairs to the kitchen and had the telephone operator ring the hospital. When someone at the hospital answered, Cow said, "This is the police. Send an ambulance to two-oh-three Maryland Avenue."

"What is the problem, officer?" the nurse asked.

Cow took a deep breath. "The resident here is dead."

"An ambulance will be there shortly."

Cow hung up the phone and then called the police station.

"Sarge, this is Cow. I'm at Jared's. You're not going to like what I found here."

"Well, then don't play games. What's the problem?"

"He's dead," Cow told the desk sergeant.

"How do you know?" Sergeant Tom Logsdon asked.

Even some of his fellow officers doubted Cow's intelligence.

Cow rolled his eyes. "Well, let's see…his face is purple and he isn't breathing. I think that's a good indication."

Ignoring the sarcasm, Sergeant Logsdon asked, "Did you take his pulse?"

Cow sighed. "I'm not going to touch him. His body is discolored. His chest isn't moving. His eyes are wide open and unblinking. He's dead."

"Any idea what happened?"

"He is still in bed. There are no signs of a struggle. It looks like he had some kind of disease. Maybe even a plague. That's why I don't want to touch him."

"You'd better hope he doesn't have the plague, Cow," the sergeant said.

"Why?"

"Because if it was a plague that killed him, you probably caught whatever he had even if you didn't touch him."

Cow began to shake so hard that he dropped the phone receiver. He sat down hard on the chair next to the phone and stared at his hands. They still looked normal. Was he going to die like Jared had?

41

Sunday, September 29, 1918

Alan closed his eyes and bowed his head as he sat in a pew in the middle of Saint Patrick's Church on Centre Street. Cumberland had a strong Catholic population filling the pews with nearly a thousand parishioners for Sunday Mass.

Catholics had held Mass on the same spot since 1791 when Saint Mary's Catholic Church had been a log cabin. When the current church had been built in 1850, it had been renamed St. Patrick's by the Irish Catholics who dominated the congregation at the time.

Emily placed her hands on her swollen belly and shifted uncomfortably on the wooden seat. Alan reached an arm behind her back and began to gently rub up and down her spine.

"That's not what's hurting and you had better not rub there while we're in church," Emily whispered.

Alan grinned.

He didn't rub where his wife was hurting. Instead, he laid a hand on Emily's belly. Was the child inside her a boy or girl? They should know by the end of the year. The baby could easily be a Christmas present this year.

"Mama, be still," Anne said, tugging on Emily's sleeve.

"Shhh," Alan told her.

"But whenever I wiggle like that, you yell at me."

"It's not Mama that's wiggling. It's your little brother or sister. He is uncomfortable being stuck inside of your mother."

Anne stared at her mother's stomach and then poked her finger into her mother's side.

"Then why doesn't he come out? Why did Mama eat him?" Anne asked.

Emily chuckled. "I didn't eat him, Anne. He's just growing there until he's ready to see you." She frowned in pain and shifted again.

Anne leaned over near her mother's belly and said, "Baby, be still." She wiggled her little fingers at her mother's belly as if the baby could see her.

For her part, Emily sighed. She settled into a comfortable position and said, "Thank you, Anne. That helped."

Alan sat back and tried to relax. It was hard to do with so many conflicting thoughts flitting through his mind. People were dying while he sat in here. Not just soldiers in the war, either. Others were dying, attacked by an unseen killer. People all over the country were suffering horrible deaths like Sarah Jenkins had. And with Sarah's death, the Spanish Flu had moved into Cumberland, or rather, it had finally made its presence in Allegany County known.

And here he sat, smiling and relaxing as if it was another fall Sunday.

Father Edward Wunder ended his Mass in Latin. Parishioners began standing in order to leave. Then Father Wunder held up his hands and began speaking in English. Father's Wunder's change in language caught Alan's attention.

"My children, as we prepare to enter October, there is also hope that this may be the last month of the Great War that has stolen so many of our husbands, fathers, brothers and sons from us. Before we leave, let us pray for the safety of those that remain at war, the defeat of the enemy and the safe return of our loved ones to us," said the priest.

There was a murmur of assent from the congregation. They sat down and bowed their heads.

Father Wunder said, "Let us pray."

The congregation bowed their heads as Father Wunder began his prayer. Alan joined in the prayer for he truly didn't want anyone more to die, American or German. But to pray for a victory and a swift end to the fighting worried him. Should God answer his prayers, wouldn't that mean the death and defeat of so many Germans, including his family who fought in the Kaiser's army?

"Please Mother Mary, I feel you understand my dilemma. You once faced making a right choice that would bring you sorrow. Though my family should not be fighting, they are and I don't want to see them die. At the same time, I don't want anyone else to have to feel what I am feeling. Please help both sides find the answer that will keep as many people alive as possible and still end the fighting," Alan prayed silently.

He sighed and wondered how much God was listening to the world when he let something like the war happen in the first place.

When the Mass was over, Alan sat in the pew. Anne tugged on his shirtsleeve.

"Come on, Papa. I want to go home. I'm hungry. I want lunch," Anne said.

Emily was also standing, waiting to go. "Is something wrong, Alan?"

Alan shrugged. "Nothing I can do anything about."

"Then why are you still sitting here?"

Alan gave his wife a half smile. "I guess I'm waiting for an answer to a prayer, but it doesn't look like one's going to come."

Emily placed a hand on his shoulder. "Why don't you go talk to Father Wunder?"

Alan patted her hand.

"Do you think that would help? He'll probably tell me the same thing you do when we talk about it," he said. He put his arms across the back of the pew in front of him and rested his head on his arms.

"Well, maybe hearing it from him will make it register with you because you're obviously not listening to me," Emily suggested.

"I am. My head agrees with you and understands you, but my heart still says I did something wrong," Alan said.

"Then go let Father Wunder talk to your heart."

Alan sighed. He stood up and nodded.

"Do you want Anne and I to come with you?" his wife asked.

Alan shook his head and handed Emily the car keys. "You two go on home. I'll walk back when I'm finished here. I'll probably want to think about what the Father says anyway."

They only lived a half a mile from the church on Columbia Street. It was a pleasant walk in the spring and the fall.

Emily kissed him on the cheek. "Just remember you are a good man who has a family who loves him and wants to see him happy again."

She took Anne's hand and waddled into the main aisle. Anne waved goodbye to Alan.

"Bye, Papa. Can you read to me when you get home?" she said.

Alan smiled. "That's a good idea. We'll do that."

Anne smiled and a warm feeling spread through Alan. He watched them walk out of the chapel and then he walked out. Father Wunder was walking inside after having said his goodbyes to the parishioners as they left the church.

He was a middle-aged man with thin, brown hair or maybe it was just his wide head that made it look like he didn't have enough hair. "Hello, Alan," he said. "Emily said you wanted to talk with me." "Yes, Father."

"Do you want to speak here or in the rectory?"

"Here would be fine. I like it in here. It helps bring me peace."

They walked back inside the church. Alan stared at the stained glass windows and sculpted ceiling. When men labored in the service of God, their works seemed twice as beautiful.

Father Wunder motioned to a front pew. Then he and Alan sat down side by side.

Alan stared at the larger-than-life statue of Christ at the front of the church. Looking at the statue usually brought him a sense of peace. That wasn't the case now. Now he felt as if Christ's gaze was condemning him. For hoping the United States was victorious against the army with whom his family fought? For hoping his family would survive even if it meant the U.S.'s defeat or some other reason Alan couldn't even discern?

"What's troubling you, my son?"

"It's the war, Father," Alan said.

Father Wunder raised his eyebrows. "It troubles everyone. Many people in this parish have fathers, brothers, husbands and sons fighting in the war. Some of them will not return and their families fear for the lives of the living. It is an uncertain time."

"I have the same fears, too, Father, but my family is fighting on the other side."

Father Wunder inhaled sharply. "Oh."

Did he draw away from Alan? Alan drew back his shoulders and sat up straighter. He had done nothing for which he should be ashamed.

"I don't want to see any harm come to them, but I certainly don't agree with Germany's position in this war. That's why I'm not back there fighting. So how do I come to terms with two differing positions like that? I'm betraying someone, but I'm not sure who it is."

Father Wunder rubbed his broad chin and then patted Alan on the thigh. "The short answer is: You aren't betraying anyone."

Alan shook his head.

"It's not your responsibility, Alan. You didn't start this war and you don't control how it is going. You didn't tell your family to fight. There should be no guilt in you. Sadness, yes, but we all feel sadness at the loss of so much life. Isn't that being a good son?"

"But my mother wanted me to come home and fight for the Kaiser. When I told her no, she and my family disowned me."

"Are you German?"

"Not any longer. I officially became an American back in May."

Father Wunder nodded. "Then the fault in your situation is your mother who is asking you to betray your new country. What you need to understand is that all things work out to God's will in the end. If it is His will for your family to die in the war, then one more soldier fighting with Germany will not change the tide. There is nothing you can do to stop that. If it is His will for Germany to lose this conflict, there is nothing you can do to change that."

"But I'm also a Kreiger."

Father Wunder put a hand on Alex's clasped hands. "Aren't any Germans Catholic?"

"Yes."

"So you have Catholics fighting on both sides of this war. One group must be wrong. It is a terrible thing to feel my brethren are in the wrong, but I know I can only play out my small part in the picture," Father Wunder explained to him.

Alan clenched the edge of the pew. "I don't know that I can accept that. Are you saying God wanted the war?"

Father Wunder's brow furrowed as he shook his head. "Certainly not. Humans, mortals, made their decisions and the consequences of those decisions are now playing out. No one knows God's will. If we think our decisions can affect God's will, we are fools. Remember the prayer: *Thy will be done.* And it will be. We can't change that.

"You must accept it. The decisions have been made and now we must deal with the results of those decisions. Certainly there will be much sadness and perhaps some of that sadness will be among your own family. You have no choice but to accept it.

"Know this, though, if your family dies innocent, they will walk with the Lord in Heaven," Father Wunder said.

"So are you saying that I'm worrying for nothing?" Alan asked.

Father Wunder looked at Alan sideways. "Can your worrying change one thing that you are worried about?"

"No."

"Then I think you answered your own question."

Alan shrugged. He may have answered his question, but it really didn't make him feel more at ease. His family might be killed and he was hoping for their defeat.

He thanked Father Wunder and walked around to the rear of the church to walk home. At least his wife and daughter were two members of his family he could keep safe.

Cow lowered his head as he walked into the police station in the basement of City Hall. He still preferred the station when it was in the old City Hall and Academy of Music. It had been a beautiful building inside and out. Cow had loved the frescoed mayor's office and stage curtain that had shown "The Decline of Carthage." It had burned down eight years ago.

As a boy, he had stood on Frederick Street, helping the firemen and crying as the building had burned in 1910. The new City Hall had been built of a paler stone and without the towers of the Academy of Music. In Cow's mind, this building was just a ghost of its predecessor.

He walked in the door and turned quickly down the hall to avoid talking to the desk sergeant. Cow wasn't sure when the ribbing would start, but he knew that it would. He only hoped to be here long enough to check in and then get back on the street where he felt more comfortable and where he wouldn't be ridiculed.

It was John Hotchkiss who started it.

Not surprising. He was a small man, both in size and personality. He thought that he was clever, but he envied Cow's size and took every opportunity to tease him.

"Hey guys, how do you get a milkshake?" he said loudly in the open room where the patrolmen had their desks.

"I don't know," someone replied. Cow wasn't sure who it was because he didn't look up. His cheeks were bright red.

"Why you just show our Cow a dead body and he'll shake for you plenty."

Cow sighed. It wasn't even a funny joke.

When the ambulance driver had come into Jared Scell's house yesterday, Cow had still been sitting on the chair in the bedroom trembling. It hadn't been the dead body that had shaken him up so much but the fact that the desk sergeant had warned him that he might have caught whatever had killed Jared. No one seemed to remember that. They just assumed that Jared had died of pneumonia.

Cow knew it was more than that. He had stared and Jared's

sprawled body and contorted face for fifteen minutes before the ambulance had arrived and he had realized that however Jared had died, it hadn't been pleasant. It had been painful and Jared had been afraid until the very end.

Cow didn't want to die that way.

No one would. Not even John Hotchkiss.

The ambulance driver must have told another police officer what he had seen and the news had spread like wildfire. Cow Lewis had been afraid of a dead body. He was a coward. He was afraid of haunts and spirits.

Maybe he deserved all the teasing. Maybe he was a coward.

Cow didn't think so. He could have run when he found the body but he had stayed. He had waited in the same room with the body. He hadn't run.

Maybe he was stupid.

Cow signed in to work and then quickly turned and headed out of the station. His beat was downtown. It was close enough to the station that he didn't need a car to get to his area. Not that there were many police cars to go around.

He paused for a few moments as he stepped outside to enjoy the silence and lack of laughter. He headed south on Centre Street, waving to some of the people along the street as he passed. He had bandaged his blisters so his feet didn't hurt.

On Baltimore Street he turned east and headed toward the railroad tracks. He paused to look in one of the many windows of McMullen Brothers. The department store dominated the whole north side of the block. Cow shopped there when he wanted something that was good quality and not too expensive. The store carried everything or so it seemed.

He stared at silk Lyons velvet and Hatters plush hats. He needed a new one with the cold coming on and now was the time to buy it.

Cow casually strolled up the block, splitting his attention between the products in the window and the people on the street. He stopped when he heard a loud voice calling out. He turned around and looked for the person he had heard shouting.

A man stood on a box at the corner of Liberty and Baltimore Street in front of the Second National Bank calling out to people as they walked by him. He wore a cheap black suit and dirty white shirt. The man must have been shouting for Cow to hear him a block and a half away.

"You were given time and what did you do with it? You squandered it! You wasted it! You embraced death and took the world to war. Now the Lord has said you will find out what truly embracing death is! Even now, the grim specter of death walks among you, preparing to make its presence known," the man called out.

Cow walked closer. He watched a few people pause to listen to the man and then shake their heads and walk off. Most people just hurried by him as quickly as they could. The man wouldn't convince too many people that fighting the Germans was not almost a holy war.

Then Cow recognized the man. He had seen him a few days ago. He'd been on Centre Street then and selling snake oil, Dr. Somebody's Elixir.

So what was he doing preaching now?

The man certainly looked paler and shakier than he had when Cow had seen him selling snake oil. Maybe he had finally realized his elixir was worthless.

The man had a street license. Cow had checked it when he'd seen the huckster on Centre Street. He couldn't do much about him now unless he started physically bothering people. And given how worked up the man was getting, that probably wasn't out of the question.

Cow would have to keep check on this man.

Monday,
September 30, 1918

When Alan walked out of the room after examining a woman who had food poisoning from her own poor cooking, he saw Peter Markwood waiting for him. The older man was agitated and a little pale.

Peter waved Alan over away from the open door. Alan didn't know what the older man wanted, but Alan could tell by his friend's creased brow that it wasn't good news.

They walked in silence a few paces down the hall away from any open doors.

"Another one came in this morning," Peter said.

"Alive?"

Peter shook his head.

Alan didn't have to ask what Peter was speaking about. They had only talked about one topic during the past week, the Spanish Flu. There had been two deaths so far that Alan and Peter were attributing to the flu. The first was Sarah Jenkins. The second corpse had come in yesterday.

Jared Scell had been a police officer. What worried Alan was that Officer Scell's death could have easily gone unnoticed. The man had been a bachelor who owned his home. There had been no reason for someone to visit him, except that he had been a police officer and he hadn't reported for work.

"Have you done the autopsy yet?" Alan asked.

Peter shook his head. "No, but there was a bloody foam around this man's mouth. That's a pretty sure sign of what we're looking for. I'll do the autopsy when I go back to the morgue. I wanted to let you know what was happening."

Alan sighed. "Who was it?"

"A man named Howard Bradbury. He ran a service station on Virginia Avenue."

Alan shook his head. "We've got a mother from Mechanic Street, a police officer from Maryland Avenue and service station owner from Virginia Avenue. If it is the flu, it's hitting without any identifiable way or in any identifiable pattern."

"Isn't that the way the flu always goes?"

Peter was a good doctor, but he was of an older generation of doctors. Germ theory had not been a part of his training. Spanish Flu almost certainly had left a trail. They just weren't seeing all of its footprints yet to know where it had been and where it was going.

Alan said, "There's always a connection. We might not be able to see it, Peter, but the same disease is not just going to suddenly appear at nearly the same time in three unconnected people. There either is a common source, contact between victims or something about those people that is the same. Most likely, we'll find lots of victims in between these victims who we already know about who survived the flue. If we can figure out the pattern, maybe we can head this outbreak off before it gets out of hand. Maybe we can help some of those people who are only sick right now."

Peter snorted. "In case, you haven't noticed, Alan, the Spanish Flu is already out of hand. It's almost like rain falling from the sky, hitting nearly everyone and making everyone it touches wet. If the flu is here and killing people, it's too late to curb it."

Alan shook his head. "No. I won't accept that."

"Alan, if we know of three deaths from influenza that probably means there are a hundred more people who have or had influenza and survived and may have passed it on to others. Who knows how many people have been infected? We're not going to be trying to prevent the flu. We're going to be trying to keep those people who have it alive."

Peter was right. Unfortunately, most people didn't check themselves into the hospital with the flu. They went to the pharmacy and bought something to treat the symptoms for a few days until they felt better.

Meanwhile, they continued to infect everyone they met.

"Can we prove it's the flu?" Alan asked.

Peter shrugged. "No. There's bacillus present in the sputum samples. At least with the first two cases. That may not mean anything since there wasn't bacillus in the spring strain. You could argue it either way."

Alan was under no illusions that the third autopsy would yield any

51

different results. It would have the bacillus.

"Can we prove that the same thing killed all three people?"

Peter thought for a moment. "I suppose so. The autopsy of Mrs. Jenkins and Officer Scell look virtually identical, as will Mr. Bradbury's, I suspect. That should be convincing that we are dealing with the same thing in all three cases, especially if the bacillus is present in all three."

Alan drummed his fingers on the plaster wall. "Okay. After you're finished the Bradbury autopsy, collect the information on all three cases. I'll put together what information I can find on the Spanish Flu and present it to Jim McAlpine."

"How can he make a decision? He's no doctor."

Jim McAlpine was a county commissioner and the acting health officer. If there were any countywide precautions to be taken, the directive would have to come from the Board of Health and Commissioner Jim McAlpine.

Alan said, "He doesn't need to be a doctor. Hyatt's a doctor and on the Board of Health, but he's denying the evidence before him. Jim's a politician. He won't want his voters to die off before they can vote for him or to blame him at the voting booth if things get out of hand because the Board of Health failed to take precautions, which is what it has done so far."

"You're being cynical," Peter noted.

"I'm searching for a way to save anymore Sarah Jenkins who might be…who are out there." Alan still worried that if he had been more astute, he would have recognized the problem with Sarah and been able to help her stay alive.

"And when Dr. Hyatt finds out you've circumvented him by going directly to McAlpine, he'll want your hide," Peter reminded him.

"Not if I'm right."

Peter offered a lopsided grin. "*Especially* if you're right."

Alan tucked the thick pile of documents under his arm and walked into the basement offices under the courthouse on Prospect Square. The county clerk sat at the desk in the front room.

Alan tried his best to look medical. He tried to imitate Dr. Hyatt.

"Is Commissioner McAlpine in? I have an appointment with him. I'm Dr. Alan Keener," Alan said.

The clerk nodded. "His office is the first door on the left."

Alan walked down the short hallway and knocked on the first office door.

"Come in," said a voice from inside the office.

Alan opened the door. County Commissioner Jim McAlpine was sitting at his desk writing a letter. He laid his pen down and leaned back in his chair. He smiled up at Alan.

"Commissioner McAlpine, I'm Dr. Alan Keener."

McAlpine nodded. "Yes, Doctor. Come in. Sit down." He waved to the chair in front of his desk.

Alan stepped inside and shut the door behind him. He didn't want someone to hear about the Spanish Flu and start a panic.

Alan sat down in one of the two wooden chairs in front of the desk. He laid his pile of papers in the second chair.

"Thank you for seeing me, Commissioner."

"From what you said, it's not Commissioner McAlpine you want to see. It's Acting Health Officer McAlpine."

Alan nodded. "Yes, there's an issue that requires the attention of the Board of Health. Have you heard about the Spanish Flu?"

Commissioner McAlpine frowned. "Nasty business from all that I've read. I wouldn't want to be living in Boston or Philadelphia right now."

Alan was glad the commissioner was familiar with the flu and what it was doing to people. The fact that he was worried about it meant he was aware of the seriousness of what Alan was going to tell him. People were dying. Part of what Alan had to do was play on that worry and feed it.

"I think the flu has made it to Allegany County," Alan said.

"What!"

The commissioner sat up straight in his chair.

Alan passed Commissioner McAlpine a letter from a doctor in Boston who had written about what an autopsy of one of the victims of the Boston outbreak showed. Alan had underlined some of the key passages that he wanted to make sure the commissioner read. It was a graphic description that would not only add to the health officer's concern, but Alan intended to build on the details the passage contained.

Jim McAlpine took the letter and read it. His eyes widened at times as they moved back and forth. He frowned and shook his head.

"This is for someone in Boston," McAlpine said after he read the letter.

"Yes, but it shows what a person who died of the Spanish Flu looks like inside. I could write up virtually the same thing about the way people in Cumberland begun dying."

McAlpine gulped but didn't say anything.

"In particular, notice that the lungs were filled with a reddish fluid, which was made up, in part, of blood. This person drowned without being in water. Not a painless way to die," Alan said.

McAlpine nodded absent-mindedly.

Alan passed the three autopsy reports of the three cases of flu death in the county. Commissioner McAlpine opened them one after the other and read through the reports.

"I knew Officer Scell. He was a good man," McAlpine said.

"Yes, sir."

Alan watched the politician's reactions. They mirrored what Alan had seen when the health officer was reading the Boston letter.

McAlpine set all of the reports aside when he had finished reading them. He looked paler than he had when he had started reading.

"Have each of these been determined to be the Spanish Flu?" McAlpine asked.

Alan nodded. "As of early this morning. I consulted with Dr. Markwood and we have made that determination."

"But are you sure?"

Sure? What did the commissioner want? A signed certificate with the cause of death listed?

"There is no test to specifically identify the Spanish Flu, sir, but the tests on the victims' tissue samples show Pfeiffer's Bacillus is present. Though Spanish Flu didn't show that last spring, the presence of the bacillus is considered an indicator of the flu."

"But it may not be an indicator of the Spanish Flu."

"We can call it the flu by the presence of the bacillus or the Spanish Flu by comparing it to other cases that it resembles. Either way, it's killing people in Allegany County. That's the important thing. Naming it means nothing. The killing is what needs to be stopped."

Commissioner McAlpine leaned back in his chair and steepled his fingers in front of his face. "This could be very serious. I've read the reports from Boston and they gave me nightmares. I am surprised that if the Spanish Flu has made an appearance in Allegany County the Board of Health hasn't heard about it."

"Doctors aren't required to report influenza to the Board of Health.

It's too common an illness, and at the same time, it's too easy to miss an outbreak if there's no general clearing house for information."

McAlpine nodded. "I realize that, but with this situation, we don't want to take any chances...and we don't want to cause a panic either," he added the last part quickly.

The commissioner was beginning to consider the various ramifications of his possible actions. He might be acting as the health officer now, but he couldn't put aside the fact that he was also a politician who wanted to be re-elected.

"Someone has to be the first to report it. I guess in this case, it is me," Alan told him.

"What does Dr. Hyatt say about this? After all, he is in charge of Western Maryland Hospital and a member of the Board of Health. Certainly you took your concerns to him?"

Alan knew he had to handle this delicately. If he disparaged Dr. Hyatt, McAlpine would probably defend the older doctor and dismiss Alan's request. If Alan lied about Hyatt's lack of support, it would come out sometime later and could derail efforts being made to prevent the flu from spreading.

Alan took a breath and said, "Quite frankly, sir, I don't think Dr. Hyatt wants to believe the Spanish Flu is here."

Commissioner McAlpine arched his eyebrows and sat forward. "Then, perhaps he has good reasons to doubt what you have seen is the Spanish Flu. He is a skilled doctor with lots of experience."

"Dr. Markwood, who also has a lot of experience, concurs with me. Dr. Hyatt hasn't seen those bodies, Commissioner. You've seen the reports. Say, I'm wrong and we're not dealing with the Spanish Flu in the city. Something killed all of those people in the same way. Flu or not, whatever it is is deadly and contagious and actions should be taken to curb it."

"As a doctor and member of the Board of Health, Dr. Hyatt would recognize that as well. He has a responsibility to the community he serves," said McAlpine.

"You are the health officer, sir. Right now, the problem is limited. A directive from the Board of Health can keep it that way."

McAlpine slowly nodded. "I am the *acting* health officer, but I do not act alone. That is why there is a *Board* of Health. I don't make my decisions alone, and if the doctors that you would like to circumvent tell me there is no problem, I will believe them because I am not a doctor."

"I am a doctor, and I have to tell you that the possibility of the Spanish Flu coming here scares me," Alan said honestly.

"It scares me as well," McAlpine agreed.

Alan leaned across the desk. "Then issue a warning to help prevent the spread. Issue precautions on how to keep yourself healthy."

"I'll bring this before the board and we will consider it."

Alan nearly collapsed on the desk. Hyatt would kill any action against the Spanish Flu if he were given the chance.

"By the time that the Board of Health debates it and decides what to do, more people will be dead," Alan said. It was a plea more than a statement.

"We will take it under consideration, doctor, but that's all I can offer you."

Alan sat back and lowered his head and slowly shook it. How many more people would die before the Board of Health decided that the threat was real?

Lucille Carter took her lunch break at one-thirty during a lull in business at the Centre Street Market. She locked the door to the market and hung a sign on the front door that said she would be back in half an hour. Then she walked next door to check on her husband.

Though John Carter would deny it, Lucille was sure that her husband was terribly sick. For the first time in forty-two years of working, John had been too ill to work this morning. John was always so healthy, but he hadn't been able to get out of bed this morning. Lucille had told him to stay in bed and he had agreed, which worried her even more than his being sick. With Frank at war, the job of keeping the market operating fell to her.

John had told her that he would be all right by morning. Lucille hadn't believed him. How would someone who had never been sick enough not to work know what needed to be done when he was too sick to work?

If John wasn't better by tomorrow, she would call Dr. Koontz and have him take a look at John. Maybe the doctor would know what to do.

Lucille walked into their home and took off her coat and gloves.

"John! John, I'm home."

Her husband didn't answer. She hoped that he wasn't napping. She would hate to wake him. Sleeping was probably the best thing for him to do right now. That was probably why he had taken sick in the first place. He was no longer twenty-five or even thirty-five years old. He was too old to be working any longer. He couldn't keep up with the hours that running his own business demanded.

She hurried into the kitchen and sliced some vegetables and beef into a pot and started a soup simmering on the stove.

With the soup cooking, Lucille walked upstairs to the bedroom to wake her husband. While sleeping was good for him, he still needed to eat. Inside the bedroom, the curtains were still drawn and the room was dark. It smelled unpleasant. Perhaps he had vomited.

"John, it's time to wake up. I've got lunch cooking for you," Lucille said.

She turned on the overhead light and saw her husband lying in bed with his eyes open.

"Why didn't you answer me? You're certainly not too sick to talk." When there was still no answer, she said, "John?"

She stepped forward and shook him by the shoulder. There was no response. His head lolled back and forth. She put her hand to his cheek and felt cold skin.

"Oh, John!" she cried.

The Spanish Flu was continuing to make its presence known in Allegany County.

Alan walked into his home and hung his coat up in the closet. He tossed his pile of paperwork onto the hallway table. All his research hadn't done him any good. Nothing had happened, and by tomorrow, Dr. Hyatt would know that Alan had been talking to Commissioner McAlpine about Spanish Flu. That would bring Alan no shortage of new problems.

"Alan, is that you?" Emily called.

"Of course. How many strange men do you have walking into the house?" he replied, forcing himself to be cheery.

"There is no one stranger than you," Emily said as she walked into the hall from the kitchen.

She kissed Alan on the cheek. He held her for a moment. He smelled the clean scent of her hair and stroked her back.

"What's the matter?" Emily asked.

"I had no luck with the Board of Health. They're not going to be proactive with this situation. They will only react when things get bad and when they do, it will far too late."

Emily squeezed him tighter. "I'm sorry."

Alan nodded. "I am, too, but not as sorry as the families of the dead will be."

What could he have done differently? Why had he failed in his effort to get Commissioner McAlpine to do something that would save lives?

He walked into the parlor and sat down in his favorite armchair. It was a padded rocking chair. He tilted his head back and closed his eyes.

"I'm making meatloaf and potatoes for dinner," Emily said.

Until she mentioned something, Alan hadn't realized how hungry he was. He hadn't eaten any lunch because he had been too nervous about his meeting with Commissioner McAlpine.

"That sounds wonderful," Alan told her.

Anne came running in and jumped into his lap. Alan grunted in surprise. They nearly toppled backwards in the chair.

"Hi, Papa."

She hugged him, gripping him in a stranglehold and Alan hugged her back, though not quite as hard as he was used to receiving.

Then Anne coughed.

Alan froze.

No. Please, no.

He put his hand on Anne's head. She was warm to the touch.

Anne had the flu.

TUESDAY, OCTOBER 1, 1918

Carson Riley woke in the early morning before the sun rose. He shivered so violently that he rattled the metal bed frame against the wall. Carson pulled his thin blanket tight around him, but it didn't bring him any relief. His teeth clattered loudly.

He sat up, clutching his blanket around his shoulders. He hurried across the cold, bare floor to the radiator. He laid his hand on it, expecting it to be cold.

Instead, it felt warm to his touch. So why was he so cold?

Carson turned around and saw the Angel of Retribution, which he had named his heavenly visitor, standing in the middle of the room. The man glowed so brightly that it was hard for Carson to stare at him. The glow must have been touched with fire because it warmed Carson's cold body.

He fell hard to the floor and bowed to the angel with his forehead on the wooden floor. He didn't even glance up as he spoke to the angel.

"What would you have me do, Master?" Carson asked, his voice trembling.

"I am pleased with your actions today. You have shown your faith and belief in the mission I have assigned to you," the angel said. His voice echoed loudly in Carson's ears.

"I do my best, Master, but so many of the people do not believe what I say."

"They will. Even now death follows behind you and soon it will make itself known to all and give truth to your words," the angel promised.

"I will do what you require of me."

"Then continue as you have, but from this point on, you shall be known as Kolas."

Carson chanced to look up and stare at the angel through squinting

59

eyes. "Why Kolas?"

"It is a word from the first language, that of Father Adam and Mother Eve. It means, 'God's wrath,'" the angel said. "Let people know you for your true purpose in life."

"Kolas?" Carson whispered. Then he smiled. He liked the sound of his name and what it meant. He would be God's tool, God's wrath. The angel had so named him.

Kolas bowed his head back down. "Thank you for the honor, Master. I will do honor to the name you have given me."

Kolas heard a knock at his door. His head jerked up and he looked at the door. When he turned back toward the angel, he stood watching Kolas silently.

He felt renewed strength at having the angel near him. He no longer felt cold either.

Kolas heard a second knock at the door.

He stood up and opened the door. A heavyset man with only a few wisps of hair on his head stood before Kolas wearing a gray bathrobe.

"Are you all right? I'm in the room below you and I heard something heavy fall on the floor," the stranger asked.

This man must have heard Kolas drop to the floor and bow to the Angel of Retribution.

"I was giving honor to an angel of God," Kolas said.

The man backed away a step. "What?"

"I was visited by an angel and received instruction from him of what God requires of me."

The stranger leaned forward and sniffed at Kolas's breath. Kolas blew gently into the man's face. Then he laid a hand on the man's head.

"The Lord's judgment be upon you," Kolas said.

The stranger jerked back.

"Don't you see the angel?" Kolas asked.

The man's eyes darted back and forth between Kolas and the empty room. "What are you talking about? I just came up to check on you."

"Do you not see the Angel of Retribution? He glows with the brightness of the sun. He brings warmth and death to this cold world."

"Fellow, I would say that you're the one who's glowing and it's not from the sun."

The man turned and walked away down the hallway, carrying with him the scent of death.

Kolas watched the man go and then looked at his hands. Did he feel younger? More powerful? Or was it that he was completely over his bout with the flu that had brought him closer to God? He turned to the angel to ask why the man hadn't seen him, but the angel was gone.

Kolas walked to the window in his room and stared down on the alley behind Baltimore Street. He saw movement as some of the merchants prepared for their stores to open. Soon, though, there would be even more people.

It was them that Kolas would stand before and warn of the wrath he would bring down upon the people of Cumberland and Allegany County like Moses killing the children of the Egyptians. Moses had warned the Egyptians and they had ignored his warning as well.

Why was it that people ignored the messengers of God?

No doubt these modern Egyptians of Cumberland would ignore the warnings of Kolas until it was too late. Kolas would strike without notice and mercy. He was God's wrath. The wicked would fall and the name of God would be exalted.

He saw the box filled with bottles of Dr. Riley's Patented Omni-Sol Elixir. He had no need for them anymore. The angel said that he would provide for Kolas's sustenance just as God had given the Israelites manna from Heaven each day during their times in the wilderness.

Kolas threw the blanket aside and dressed himself in his best suit to prepare for the day. He chose a black broadcloth suit, white shirt, black vest and string tie. When he had finished, Kolas studied himself in the small mirror. He looked almost like a preacher. He felt that was quite appropriate, as he was an emissary bringing death to the people of Cumberland, then Allegany County, and then the world.

Lorene Sears walked aimlessly down Mechanic Street, the letter she had received this morning dangled unnoticed in her right hand. Twice, a car braked suddenly and beeped its horn at her because the young woman wandered into the road without looking to see if there was traffic approaching.

Though a cold wind blew from the north, she wore only a blue sweater, which was unbuttoned and flapped in the wind like two wings. Underneath the sweater, she only wore a thin blouse. She didn't even notice the cold. She felt nothing.

The tears were gone from her freckled cheeks, but her eyes were still red from crying for the last half an hour.

61

Lorene turned up Baltimore Street without bothering to pause to look in the windows of the stores on the first floor of the new Fort Cumberland Hotel that had opened in January. She had no destination in mind. She wasn't even sure where she was.

Lorene finally stopped walking to lean against a lamp post. She lifted the letter and read it once again. It was a letter from a soldier named Thomas Hannity, who had served with Lorene's fiancé, Robert Harkin at Camp Meade near Annapolis. The two of them had stood together in the various lines where soldiers were put in alphabetical order and they had become friends. The letter was short and explained Robert had caught the flu last week after only three weeks at the camp. He had died two days ago. Robert wasn't the only soldier who had died at the camp and all of the soldiers were worried that they would also fall victim next. The letter also said that Robert's personal effects, including the framed picture of Lorene he had kept near his bunk, would be sent to his parents in Cumberland.

Lorene closed her eyes, expecting tears to come. None did. She was cried out.

It was wrong. There should be more tears. Robert was gone. Her life was gone.

She and Robert were supposed to be married in two months, but then he had been drafted a month ago. Lorene had supported him, though, because he was doing his duty for his country. She had to do hers and let him go. Lorene even thought she had steeled herself should he die in battle.

But to die from the flu?

People got the flu every year, but she never knew anyone who had died from it.

What was she going to do now? Robert had been her future and now she was gone.

Lorene walked up the street in a daze for a few more feet and then looked at the letter as if it was the first time she had seen it. She crossed Liberty Street, barely missing walking into the side of a car that was driving along Liberty Street.

How could Robert be dead? It wasn't fair! He only wanted to help his country.

"He has asked for peace and you have only brought war. Now He will show you who truly has the power of life and death!"

Lorene blinked and looked up at the sound of the booming voice.

She looked around and finally saw the man who was speaking, standing in front of St. Paul's Lutheran Church another block ahead of her. She stopped moving and listened. She could hear every word he said even above the traffic and crowd noise.

"Now it is too late for most of you. The decision has been made and Kolas will sweep you away like fallen leaves. The Lord's judgment will fall upon you and only a few will survive. Those who follow Kolas and become a part of God's wrath may live."

Something about the man's voice tugged Lorene forward. She gathered with the small group of people that were standing around the dark-haired man at the corner of Centre and Baltimore Streets. His eyes were wide and fiery. They were magnets that pulled those who stared at them toward the man.

"Come forward and find out if you are accepted as a tool of God or one who will be burned away like chaff in the field! Discover if you have a future or your life ends through Kolas."

Future? Lorene had no future and she knew that.

No one moved forward to accept the challenge, but someone called out, "What will you do?"

The preacher smiled and said, "Nothing you need fear if you are the chosen of God. However, if you are not, then you shall be marked by Kolas."

"What's Kolas?"

"Kolas is God's wrath. I am Kolas. I am God's wrath."

Lorene stepped forward. She was not afraid of death. She had no future. "Kill me, then."

"Are you so sure you will die then, my child?" Kolas asked.

Lorene stared into Kolas's fiery eyes. "I've got nothing to live for."

"What if you are chosen to be a tool such as I am? Do you accept your destiny? Will you serve God and spread his wrath?"

Lorene simply shrugged and waited. She clutched her letter in both hands and held it in front of her as if it would be a protection.

Kolas leaned his head back. "Then let the test begin."

He licked his thumb and then traced a cross on Lorene's forehead. She winced at his touch but held steady. Then Kolas drew back satisfied.

"Is that all?" Lorene asked. "What happened? I'm still alive."

She had felt nothing except the moisture on her head.

"Wait and see. Death will find you through the mark of Kolas. If you are alive in the three days, you will know God has chosen you to serve him. If you are dead, then his wrath will have begun."

Lorene shook her head, disoriented. "So what do I do now?"

"Go home. Find me again in three days and we will talk."

Lorene turned and walked away, still in a daze. She walked back across Baltimore Street, still staring at Kolas. He watched her go, nodding slowly.

Kolas turned back to the small gathering of people. "There is nothing to fear if you are among the chosen, but even the chosen will die if they have not been marked by Kolas. Join me now as that young lady has done. Only then may you live."

Lorene paused in front of the S.T. Little Jewelry Store, ignoring the necklaces and rings on display in the window, she lifted the letter to read it again.

Robert was gone and she hoped that she would be joining him in a few days.

WEDNESDAY, OCTOBER 2, 1918

Alan stood in the doorway to the bedroom staring at his daughter lying on her bed. She had curled herself up into a tiny ball under the blankets. Her body shook so much that Alan could see the movement it in the dark room.

At least she's moving, Alan told himself.

Although the sun was rising, it wasn't showing itself yet through the window because Anne's room overlooked the narrow alley between the Keeners' home and the Brooks's house next door.

Anne stirred uncomfortably under her quilt. Alan was amazed she hadn't kicked it off since her hair was damp with sweat. His daughter looked like a small burrowing mole as she tried to get comfortable in her sleep.

She's getting worse.

Steam radiators heated the room, but not to the point where Anne should be sweating. The temperature felt comfortable to Alan. But not Anne. Her body burned up with a fever.

Alan shivered, not from cold but from fear. The small hairs on his neck rose as if death breathed on his neck and whispered, "She's mine."

He leaned his head against the doorframe and tried to keep from crying. This couldn't be happening! Why had God helped him become a doctor only to place him in a position where he his skills proved worthless to those who mattered the most to him?

"Is this the answer to my prayer, God?" Alan whispered. "Are you taking an eye for an eye?"

Was this how Sarah Jenkins had died in one night? Had her symptoms accelerated at a breakneck speed to carry her into death's waiting arms in the lonely hours between dusk and dawn?

Despite her cough, Anne had seemed fine yesterday. Alan had

65

hoped that his worries that Anne had Spanish Flu had been overblown. Then this morning, Anne had complained that she "hurt all over." Emily had given her aspirin and orange juice and put her to bed.

Anne's symptoms had only gotten worse through the evening. Emily hadn't seemed concerned. She hadn't made the connection that Alan had made. The quick escalation of the symptoms had only confirmed to Alan that Anne had the Spanish Flu. He hadn't said anything to Emily. She would assume the worst and he had hoped that he was mistaken. He kept telling himself that he was tired and seeing Spanish Flu in every shadow. Anne simply had a bad cold.

By the time he had put her to bed earlier, her fever had started.

Alan hadn't slept because he was afraid that his only child would die during the night. He had sat in the chair by her bed and watched her. When she had slept peacefully at first, Alan had begun to feel relief that he had been mistaken. He had even managed a few hours of sleep in the chair.

Then around four o'clock in the morning he had awakened to his daughter's moaning. He'd opened his eyes and found Anne like this.

Feverish.

Sick.

Dying.

How fast would her symptoms progress? What could he do? The telegram from Baltimore had given him little hope at being able to stem the course of the symptoms, but there had to be a way.

He couldn't let his only child die.

Not everyone who caught the Spanish Flu died from it. If Alan could just keep Anne alive, the flu would run its course in two or three days. He just had to keep her alive for seventy-two more hours and she would be fine.

He looked at his watch. It was seven o'clock Wednesday morning. Saturday morning would tell the tale. He had to keep her alive until then.

"What's wrong?"

Alan looked up and saw Emily standing in the doorway to their bedroom. Her swollen belly poked out between the sides of her bathrobe because the robe wasn't large enough to stretch all the way around a pregnant woman.

"Anne's sick," Alan said.

"What's wrong?"

Emily hurried across the hall and started into Anne's room. Alan reached out and held his wife back. She struggled to get past him.

"What are you doing? Let me go to her!" Emily said. Her voice was on the edge of sobbing.

He couldn't let her get close to Anne right now. He couldn't take a chance that Emily would catch the flu, too. Her system was already sustaining two lives. He couldn't endanger her by allowing her to get infected and become as sick as Anne.

"You can't go to her until we know what's wrong," Alan said.

"Why not? I'm her mother!"

"It may be the flu," Alan said simply.

Emily paused and her eyes went wide. "The flu? But...do you mean the flu that you are...oh, no. Not Anne! You're wrong. She doesn't have the Spanish Flu."

Emily tried to push past Alan again, but he remained in front of her. He couldn't let her near Anne until he knew for sure that his daughter was not contagious.

"I hope I'm wrong, Emily, but she's not getting any better," Alan said.

"But it doesn't have to be the Spanish Flu. It could be something else."

"There are not different types of flu going around at once. If she has the flu this season, she has the Spanish Flu variation."

Emily sagged against Alan and cried. Alan hugged her gently and then turned her around. He led her back to their bedroom and tucked her into her bed.

"Not Anne. She can't be sick. She's so young, Alan," Emily cried.

"Not everyone who gets the flu dies, Emily. Most people survive the flu, even the Spanish Flu," Alan told her. He heard himself say the words and it sounded like a weak hope even to him.

"But too many people are dying. I read the newspapers. It scares me. I know how bad it is and now it's coming here."

No, she didn't know how bad it was. She hadn't seen the autopsies. She hadn't read the health reports that Alan had seen. Alan prayed that Cumberland didn't become a mass grave like Philadelphia or Boston were quickly becoming. Those cities had thousands of people dying. The dead were piling up in the morgues because there were too many bodies and not enough undertakers to bury them all.

He had to kill the bacillus, but how? Gargles and antiseptic swabs had proven ineffective in other cities. No one had found a treatment that worked.

"I want to take Anne to the hospital," Alan said.

"Is she that bad already?"

Alan tried to smile. "She's sick and I want to make sure she doesn't get sicker. If she's at the hospital, I can watch her closely and make sure she gets healthy."

And as she got sicker, he would be in a position to help her with the hospital equipment and medicines at his disposal.

"If you take her to the hospital, she'll be all right?"

Alan hesitated. "I don't know."

Emily sobbed silently and shook her head. She reached out and grabbed hold of Alan's arm.

"Is she going to die?"

Alan knew the answer that his wife wanted to hear, but it wasn't the truth. He didn't know if his daughter was going to live or die. If he told Emily that Anne would be fine, how would she react if she died? How would he react?

He sighed and said, "I just don't know, Emily, but I would rather her be in the hospital where I can care for her. The medicines are there. The nurses are there to watch her around the clock."

"She's five years old, Alan. She needs her mother."

Emily started to sit up in the bed, but Alan pushed her back.

"Anne needs medical attention," Alan said. "You getting sick, too, won't help her or the baby."

Resistance seemed to flow out of Emily's body and she relaxed back into the bed. She rubbed her hands around her belly as if she was trying to sense what the baby wanted her to do. She didn't say anything, but Alan took the action as an acceptance of his argument.

Alan walked into the bathroom and quickly showered and shaved. He had to slow down as he lathered his face when he realized that his hand was shaking. He didn't want to slice his throat open.

When he came back out, he saw Emily sitting on Anne's bed, holding her and stroking her brow. Emily cradled her daughter in her arms and rocked back and forth.

"Emily!"

Emily looked up. There was a deep sadness in her eyes. Her cheeks were streaked with the trails of dried tears.

"She's very sick, Alan."

Alan nodded. "I know. You need to come away from there before you get the same sickness. You've got to take care of yourself."

When Emily stood up, Anne whimpered and reached out for her. Emily leaned toward her daughter but Alan pulled her back. He took his wife by the arm and led her from the bedroom.

"I wanted to say goodbye to her before you take her away," she said sadly.

Goodbye.

That sounded so final. It almost sounded as if Emily had given up her daughter for dead already. Alan wasn't going to let his daughter die.

He led his wife back to bed. He tucked her into bed and kissed her on the forehead. He dressed and looked back at Emily. She was crying again. He only wished that he could say something to ease her worries. The only way to do that was to get his daughter healthy again.

"I'm going to get Anne dressed. Then I'll get her to hospital and run a few tests. Maybe it's something other than the flu," Alan said.

They both knew differently, though. Anne had the Spanish Flu.

Alan checked his daughter's temperature while she lay in the hospital bed. It was still over 100 degrees. Her face was flushed red. She didn't show any signs of improving and now she was having trouble breathing. He could hear the fluid in her lungs when he listened to her chest with a stethoscope.

Alan actually felt a pain in his chest each time he looked at his daughter.

Since he had brought her into the hospital, he had immediately begun trying different treatments he had heard of for treating Spanish Flu. He had had Anne gargle with a disinfectant and was applying Vick's VapoRub to her chest to ease her breathing. He knew they were useless treatments, but he had to try something. Anything.

Alan had her trying to cough up phlegm or fluid from her lungs. He wanted to keep her lungs as clear of fluid as he could. That was the key. If her lungs filled with fluid, she would drown like Sarah Jenkins had died. He too clearly remembered the engorged red lungs he had seen during Sarah's autopsy.

He had taken to wearing gloves and a mask in Anne's room because he was sure that she had the flu no matter how much he wanted to deny it.

"Papa, I want Mama," Anne said weakly.

Dark circles had formed under her eyes from her lack of sleep. Sweat plastered her brown hair to her head. She looked so worn out and beaten. Where was his little girl who had laughed and played only a day ago?

Alan nodded. "I know you want your mama, Anne, but you're sick right now. If Mama gets too close to you, she might get sick, too."

Anne started crying. "I don't like it here. It's scary. You look scary like a robber."

Alan pulled a chair over next to her bed and sat down. He ran his gloved fingers through her brown hair. He could feel the heat emanating from her head as her body fought the fever.

"I know you're scared, darling, but you have to stay here until you get better. We're trying to make you feel better."

Alan heard a knock at the door and turned around. Helen stood there looking nervous.

"Dr. Hyatt asked to see you," the nurse said. Then she added, "He didn't look happy."

Alan nodded. "Fine. I'll be there in a moment."

Alan turned back to Anne. She was still crying. He wiped the tears away with his gloved hand.

"I have to go, darling, but I'll be back," he said.

Anne shook her head. "Don't leave me here. I'm scared."

"It will be all right. I'm not leaving the hospital. It's like I'll be in another room of a big house. I'll come back and check on you as soon as I see Dr. Hyatt," he promised. He smiled at her and brushed her damp hair back off her forehead.

Then he pulled off his facemask and kissed Anne on the forehead. The kiss tasted slightly of salt from her perspiration.

Alan stood up and walked out of the room. As he walked down the hallway, he pulled his mask from around his neck. He took off his rubber gloves and shoved them into his pockets. It was all he could do to keep himself from crying.

The door to Dr. Hyatt's office was open when he reached it. Dr. Hyatt saw him coming and waved him inside. Dr. Hyatt sat back in his desk chair and frowned.

"Come in, doctor, and close the door behind you," Dr. Hyatt said.

Alan did as he asked. When Dr. Hyatt didn't offer him a chair, Alan remained standing, though he was tired from being up most of the night.

"I received an interesting phone call this morning. Commissioner McAlpine has called an emergency meeting of the Board of Health to talk about the presence of the Spanish Flu in our county. Now I wonder why he is so worried about that," Hyatt said.

Alan said nothing.

Hyatt was working his anger up. Alan had no desire to trigger it early. His own anger was building, too. How dare Hyatt take him away from Anne just to scold him about something so petty as to who got the Board of Health to act!

"But you know why he is upset, seeing as how you visited him yesterday and laid out your argument to him," Hyatt added.

The older doctor stood up and slowly began to pace the room. "Dr. Keener, you are a doctor in my hospital and I am a member of the Board of Health. If you have a concern about a county health issue, the proper procedure is to come to me..."

"I did come to you," Alan finally said.

Hyatt held up a hand to silence him. "The proper procedure is to come to me and I will decide whether the issue needs to be taken to the Board of Health."

"As a citizen of the county, I have the right to present any issue I feel needs to be presented to my county officials," Alan said.

It sounded like a weak excuse to Alan even as he said it. While it might be true, it wasn't the truth, which is probably why it sounded so weak.

Hyatt snorted. "I forgot you are Mr. New American. Well, I have lived in this country all my life as my father did and his father did. We are real Americans and we know how things work here. You work at this hospital and I run this hospital. You work under me and as such, if you have an issue involving this hospital, then you come to me!" Hyatt's soothing "concerned doctor" tone had evaporated.

Alan shook his head, feeling frustrated at having to defend himself about this issue to another doctor. "You don't understand what's happening, do you? Spanish Flu doesn't involve just this hospital. Those people who have died haven't died in this hospital. They are dying out in the city and county. That's where the issue is. This isn't about you and your authority. This is about keeping people alive."

Alan walked around the desk and grabbed Hyatt by the arm. The muscle was surprisingly thick under the suit.

"What are you doing?" the older man asked, shocked.

Hyatt tried to pull his arm free but Alan held him tight.

"Come with me. I'll show you where the issue involves this hospital," Alan snapped.

"I'll have your job for this," Hyatt threatened.

"I don't care at this point, but you are going to come with me or I will drag you down the hallway. Then what will people think about you?"

Hyatt stood up and smoothed out his suit. "Fine. I will come with you to where you want and then you will leave this hospital."

Alan set his expression in a scowl and pointed to the door to Hyatt's office. Hyatt walked around his desk to the door. He paused there and looked over his shoulder. Alan thought the man would say something, but Hyatt opened the door and walked out.

Alan led Hyatt to the door of his daughter's room.

"Look in there," Alan said.

Hyatt opened the door and saw Anne. She had fallen asleep, but her breathing was strained and hoarse. He could hear the gurgle of fluid in each breath she took. She looked paler than when Alan had left her. He wanted to cry, but he had to be hard to face Hyatt. The older doctor watched for a few moments and then closed the door.

"That is my daughter. She has the Spanish Flu, which you don't believe exists in Allegany County, and if she dies from that non-existent disease, I will hold you responsible." Alan leaned in closer to Hyatt. "And if I hold you responsible, I will make sure that you are the next one who catches this non-existent flu." There was no emotion in his voice just cold anger.

Hyatt pushed Alan away. "Now don't be rash, Alan. I can see you are upset right now and I understand why. I can also see some type of illness is spreading. I'm not blind. You stay here and treat your daughter and I'll make sure that the Board of Health looks into the matter. We'll contact other boards and get their advice on how to best handle this."

Alan relaxed and stared at Hyatt. Then he turned and leaned his head against the wall.

"I'm sorry to threaten you, Dr. Hyatt, but that's my daughter in there. She's only five years old. Five years old! She's so young and I'm afraid that she might die."

Hyatt put a hand on Alan's shoulder. "At my age, they all seem too young and they are when it comes to death."

Hyatt patted Alan's shoulder and then walked away. Alan walked back into the room with his daughter. He put his gloves and mask on and sat down next to her bed.

He checked Anne's temperature every hour. It remained high and her breathing became more labored. He raised the end of her bed to make her feet higher than her head, hoping that it would help her breathe easier. After two hours, he could tell no difference. If anything, her breathing was more labored as her lungs filled with fluid.

If Anne couldn't rid herself of the fluid, she would drown like Sarah Jenkins had. She would die struggling to breathe, inhaling with all of her strength but pulling in no air because there was no place for it to go.

Around three o'clock in the afternoon, Anne opened her eyes and stared at Alan.

"Hi, sweetheart," he said.

"Papa, I can't feel my feet," she whispered.

Alan closed his eyes momentarily and forced himself not to cry. He had to be strong. He had to be calm.

He smiled. "They're still there. Both of them."

"But I can't feel them."

Alan stroked her brow. "It's all right, Anne. You're just tired."

She nodded weakly and closed her eyes. When Alan was sure she was asleep, he lifted the sheet and looked at Anne's feet. They were covered in black spots where the tissue had begun to die because it wasn't getting enough oxygen.

Just like Sarah Jenkins.

Alan let the sheet fall and he dropped into the chair. He leaned against the side of the bed and cried silently. He was now on a deathwatch.

A nurse found Alan when she made her rounds at eight o'clock in the evening. He was lying in bed with his daughter, cradling her in his arms. The nurse started to step back out of the room and then stopped. She stared at the two of them lying on the bed.

She moved forward and touched Anne Keener on the brow. The nurse sighed. The girl's skin was cool. Her fever had broken.

The nurse placed her hand under the girl's nose. She didn't feel anything.

The nurse shook Alan's shoulder.

"Dr. Keener?"

Alan opened his eyes. He sat up.

"What is it?"

The nurse hesitated, but she glanced at Anne. Alan saw the look and drew back to look at Anne. His eyes widened and he put his fingers on his daughter's neck. He couldn't feel a pulse. He shut his eyes and his hand dropped away.

"Oh, Anne."

He pulled his daughter to him and cried. He had known this moment was coming, but it came too soon. He hadn't been able to ready himself. His daughter had only had the flu! All he had to do was keep her alive for seventy-two hours and she would be fine. Why couldn't he do that? She shouldn't be dead.

"Doctor, what should I do?" the nurse asked.

Alan looked up and stared at her for a moment as if he was trying to focus on her face. He took a deep breath and pulled himself away from Anne. He laid her gently on the bed and pulled the blanket up to her chin. He stepped back and he looked her.

"Her name is Anne," Alan said quietly.

"I know, doctor. Should I call someone? Should I call you a taxicab?"

"No."

He turned and walked out of the hospital room. He didn't even put his coat on as he walked outside into the cold night air.

His daughter was dead. How could that be?

How could an unseen virus kill so many innocent people? This was not a war zone half a world away. This was Cumberland!

But it was a war. It was a war against the flu, a war against death.

How could a war like that be won?

So many medical advances had been made during the war that there must have been new methods and new drugs that could help in this battle. Still, the army didn't seem to be doing any better in combating the Spanish Flu than civilians were.

The answer was out there. Alan just had to find it.

He walked up the half a dozen stairs to his front porch, moving slower with each step. He walked into the house.

Emily was sitting in the parlor, sewing trim on a dress for Anne. The fabric was spread out across her swollen belly. She looked up as he entered.

"You're late," she said.

Alan nodded.

"How's Anne?"

Alan opened his mouth to say something, but no words came out. All he could do was shake his head.

Emily clenched her eyes shut and sobbed.

Alan hurried to her and put his arm around her shoulders and they cried together.

Thursday
October 3, 1918

Nancy Costello had taught third grade at Pennsylvania Avenue School in South Cumberland for the past three year. She earned fifty dollars a month and all the satisfaction she could handle. She loved seeing the expressions on her young students' faces when understanding finally dawned on them. It was an understanding she had led those young minds to find and it was work she took seriously.

As Nancy wrote out math problems in chalk on the blackboard, the numbers blurred and doubled. She blinked, hoping to realign the numbers. Then she backed away a step and rubbed her eyes. When she opened them again, the room swirled around her.

She steadied herself with a hand on the edge of her desk. The desk seemed to move under her so she grabbed the sides of the desktop with both her hands. Nancy felt as if she was burning up.

Her students watched her, waiting for their instructions. Nancy saw them but she couldn't focus on them. They looked blurry. She blinked a few times, afraid to rub her eyes for fear she would fall if she let go of the desk. The number of students doubled and then shrank back to one.

"I...I need to see the Principal Boughton," Nancy said.

She took four staggering steps toward the door to her room and collapsed. She was so delirious it didn't even hurt when her nose broke as she hit the wooden floor. She didn't even hear her children's screams of fear as they watched her fall and not get up.

Across town, Ross Brandenburg washed the fire engine in Station No. 3 in Spruce Alley on the west side of Cumberland. The B&O tracks ran behind the station and coal dust filled the air at all hours of the day. It changed the red engine to a dull gray unless Ross kept it washed so it gleamed.

He paused in his work and wiped his forehead with the back of his hairy forearm. He was surprised he had worked up such a sweat. It wasn't as if he was working all that hard. When he finished the engine, he would start on the windows of the two-story station. Coal dust also kept them particularly cloudy.

Ross's head began to throb a few minutes later while he polished the brass alarm bell. The pain became so bad that he stopped his work and went into the station in search of aspirin.

Spanish Influenza had found fertile ground in Cumberland.

Anne's small body was laid out in Louis Stein's Funeral Home on North Center Street. Alan found himself grateful that the dead were generally no longer displayed in the parlors of their homes. He was not sure how he could have dealt with his the constant sight of his daughter's body every time he walked through the parlor of his house. It would have ripped his soul apart every time he saw her. It was hard enough to be in the house and know he would never hear his daughter's laughter again.

The main floor of Stein's Funeral Home held the offices, reception room and a chapel. A morgue and embalming room that most people didn't know about occupied the rear of the house. Right now, Alan wished his work as a doctor hadn't given him an understanding of what went on in those rooms; what had gone on with his daughter. The second floor had an additional reception area and casket parlor and the third floor had storage and work areas.

Alan and Emily spent Thursday morning making the funeral arrangements for Anne with Louis Stein. He was a kind man about sixty years old with graying hair and mustache. He wore round glasses that drew attention to his sad eyes.

Emily had seemed calm and rational throughout the meeting. She picked out a casket for her daughter as if she was selecting fruit at the market. She also seemed oddly detached from everything. Her eyes had a slightly glazed over look as if she saw things without really focusing on them. She talked as if a part of her was somewhere else.

After making preparations at the funeral home, Alan and Emily spent most of the afternoon dealing with the visits of friends and family at home. The visits also helped occupy them and keep the two of them from continually dwelling on the fact that one small voice was missing from the conversations.

Alan found that he expected his daughter to come charging up to

77

him. He would look around for his daughter and then realize that the dead girl they were talking about was Anne. Then tears would fill his eyes once again.

Emily's parents were there, sharing in her grief. Alan's mother-in-law cried. She and Emily hugged nearly continuously, their tears soaking each other's shoulders.

Alan's father-in-law, Howard Beall, stared accusingly at Alan as if blaming him for Anne's death...or rather, blaming Alan for not saving the life of the little girl Grandpa Howard doted on.

Alan could not meet his father-in-law's stare because Alan knew Howard was right. Alan had failed his daughter.

Alan tried to ignore him and speak with the other visitors. Most people offered their sympathies and recalled their memories of Anne. How she had skipped through the neighborhood singing made-up songs. How she had picked flowers to give to people even if they weren't hers to pick. How she would sit on her porch in the evenings and wave to the drivers who passed by on the street.

Other people steered the conversation away from Anne. They wanted to pretend as if she had never lived rather than face the fact that she had lived and died. Alan refused to be dissuaded. He wanted to remember his daughter as she had been. He would never forget. Never.

"What is happening in this world, Alan, if God can take a young girl like Anne?" said Isaac Johansen, Alan's next-door neighbor.

"God didn't take her. The flu did," Alan said as he stared at the casket.

Her small body looked so frail. The funeral make-up gave her the appearance of a porcelain doll. As unnatural as she looked, she looked far better than she had in the hospital bed as she lay dying.

But at least she had been alive.

Isaac nodded. "And that's another thing. What is happening to this city? People are sick everywhere and they're dying."

"It's not just Cumberland. This is happening across the country. It's an epidemic." Alan had seen more reports today. It was terrifying how many people were dying.

Alan walked a few steps away from the casket. Then he turned himself so that he was still looking in the direction of the casket. Isaac followed him and stood next to him.

"Since when do people die from the flu?" Isaac asked.

Alan shrugged. "It happens, Isaac. If it didn't, we wouldn't be here. My daughter wouldn't be dead. We're fighting something that can't be seen."

Isaac put a hand on Alan's shoulder. "I know you did what you could to save her, Alan, but what if it's meant to be?"

Alan frowned. Mass deaths were never meant to be. "What do you mean?"

"Well, this flu is not acting like any other flu that you doctors have ever had to deal with. It defies treatment by any type of modern medicine. It's not natural."

"Of course it's natural."

Isaac shook his head. His voice became soft enough so it was a whisper in a room of whispers. "Maybe there's something else involved here. There's been someone talking downtown by the bank, a street preacher, I guess, who says this is the wrath of God."

"No!" Alan said more sharply than he intended. Some of the people nearby stopped their quiet conversations and looked up at him.

Alan could not see God's hand in this. Why would God be angry with Anne? She had been a joy, a delight, and a testament to what mankind could be. God could not be that cruel.

"I'm just telling you what the preacher's saying. He's got people listening to him, too. He makes sense," Isaac cautioned.

"Why would they do that?"

Isaac looked at him like he was crazy. "Because they're scared. They don't want to get sick and die from something they can't see in order to avoid it," Isaac said.

Alan shook his head. "Foolish."

Alan looked over at his wife. She lifted her head from her mother's shoulder and stared back. She looked pale from the strain of recent events.

Alan hoped that Isaac didn't speak with Emily this weekend. The last thing she needed to hear was that her daughter had been killed as a victim of God's wrath. Besides being utterly foolish, it was hurtful and Emily had been hurt enough already.

He watched as Emily smiled weakly and then glanced at the casket. The smile slid away and she aged twenty years in two seconds.

She pushed herself out of her chair with great effort and walked to the casket. She had made the same journey multiple times this evening. She had gone to the casket far more times than Alan had. He just couldn't bring himself to look at his dead daughter. She didn't look natural to him with embalming fluid in her veins and make-up on her face. He didn't want to remember her that way. He wanted to remember her alive and vibrant, running and playing.

Emily waddled to the casket and leaned heavily against it. The casket swayed slightly on the hidden stand. She cried silently and laid her hand on Anne's cheek. Then she suddenly slipped to her knees and fell over on her side.

Alan rushed to Emily's side and lifted her head.

"Emily!"

She was unconscious. He put his fingers to her throat. Her pulse beat fast.

"Someone help me get her to the car. I need to get her to the hospital," Alan said.

The men in the room hurried forward and half a dozen pairs of hands helped Alan gently lift his wife and carry her out to their car. They laid her in the rear seat.

"Do you need me to come along and help you get her into the hospital?" Isaac asked.

Alan shook his head. "No, Isaac. The nurses can help me once we're there. Thank everyone for coming for me, if you would."

Isaac nodded that he would.

Alan started the car and quickly drove the short distance to the hospital. He pulled up in front of the emergency entrance. He climbed out of the car and ran inside.

"I need some help! I've got a sick woman here!" Alan called.

Two nurses came outside with Alan. They brought a gurney with them. Emily was still unconscious. They lifted her onto the gurney.

"Isn't this your wife?" Nurse Katherine McKinley asked.

"Yes," Alan said quickly.

"Is she in labor?"

"No, she collapsed during Anne's viewing. Get her into an examining room and I'll take a look at her," Alan said.

The nurses wheeled the gurney through the double doors into the hospital. Once inside, Alan leaned against the wall and caught his breath. He needed to clear his head. He needed to be able to think straight and concentrate. Emily's life depended on it. He couldn't fail her like he had Anne.

If anything happened to Emily…

He took a deep breath and walked down the hallway not far behind the gurney. The nurses would have Emily on the examining table by the time Alan got there.

"What brings you here, Alan?"

Alan looked up and saw Lucas Shearer, one of the doctors at the hospital. Lucas was a rotund man who was five inches shorter than Alan, which only gave him a rounder look.

"Emily collapsed at the viewing. I drove her here to get examined," Alan said with a sigh.

"Emily?" Lucas said, surprised. "She is the one who was just admitted?"

Alan nodded.

"It's not the flu, is it?"

Lucas actually turned pale. Alan wondered what the man would do if the flu reached epidemic proportions in Cumberland like it had in Philadelphia.

"Good Lord, I hope not. I'm going to check her out," Alan said.

"Do you need help?" Lucas had posed the question tentatively, his duty as a doctor overcoming his fear of the flu.

Alan shook his head and put a hand on Lucas's shoulder. "No, but thank you. I can handle this."

Alan turned and walked into the examining room and saw that Emily had regained consciousness.

"What happened, Alan? Where am I?" she asked. She looked worried and on the verge of crying again. She also looked pale except for the dark circles that were forming under her eyes.

"You fainted and collapsed at the funeral home," he said as he sat down on the stool next to the bed.

He took her wrist in his and timed her pulse. It was slower now than it had been at Stein's, but he still thought it was too fast.

"I'm so tired. I haven't slept at all since Anne...died," she said.

"I still want to check you out anyway. Hopefully all you need is rest and sleep."

Alan put his stethoscope on and listened to the heartbeat of his child in Emily's womb. It was fast, but no faster than normal. He felt Emily's stomach for movement. There was some, but it didn't seem like it was as much as it usually was. Had the baby been hurt when Emily collapsed or was it asleep?

"Emily, I want you to stay here at least overnight," he said.

"Why? Is something the matter?"

She tried to sit up, but he put his hands on her shoulders to push her down.

"No. Nothing is wrong, and I want to make sure it stays that way. I'm going to give you some warm milk to help you sleep and I need you to sleep. You've got to think about the baby."

"Is the baby in danger?"

Alan shook his head. "I don't think so. Your problem is exhaustion, but if you don't take care of yourself, there could be complications."

He patted her hand and then left to get her the milk. He was tempted to put something else in it, but anything stronger might harm the baby. It would have to be milk only and Emily would have to find a way to rest.

Chief Oscar Eyerman stepped in front of the room of officers. Being average height and nearing forty years old, he was not an imposing man, but he was a man in command. And he was a man with a mission.

He had served on the Cumberland City Council in 1914 as the street commissioner. Then, running unopposed, he was elected as police commissioner in 1916. He had served in that position for a year and a half until he felt compelled to take a more-active role in law enforcement. He had become chief of police earlier this year and was now facing his first crisis of command.

Dressed in his blue-cloth uniform and blue-cloth helmet, Eyerman looked like a leader. He lifted his helmet off and set it on the podium in front of him. He looked at the twenty-two officers but he didn't smile.

Cow Lewis squirmed in his seat. The chief didn't call meetings of the entire department often. Something bad must have happened, which didn't bode well for Cow. Bad news usually meant more work for the police and sometimes more danger.

"Gentlemen, we are facing a problem. The Spanish Influenza has reached Cumberland. How many of you have been reading about it?"

A few hands went up. Cow's hand was not one of them. Working twelve-hour shifts, he never had time to read the newspaper most days.

"You all have a right to know what's going on because you will be on the front lines of this epidemic. Spanish Influenza is very contagious and very deadly. There is very little anyone can do at this point to stop it. The Board of Health is considering what can be done and we will act on their advice. However, we've already been hit with it. Jared Scell was killed by the flu. That is how dangerous it is," Eyerman explained.

Cow froze. Scell was killed by the flu? A contagious flu? Then that meant Cow might have it. He might die like Scell had! The image of Scell's body sprawled across his bed with his features twisted in pain flashed in his mind. Cow shivered.

"If we can't do anything about it, then why tell us?" George Ferguson, a patrolman, asked.

Chief Eyerman said, "Because it's going to cause problems. You are going to find people dead and not know what happened to them. You will see no signs of foul play, but you will find patches of black or deep-blue skin on their bodies. This means you are probably looking at a victim of the flu. People will be sick and scared and they will be turning to us for help. We need to be ready. As I am given the precautions we can take, I will pass them on. That is all for now."

The chief turned and left the room. Everyone sat in silence. How do you fight death?

Cow realized that he was now not the only police officer who was afraid of what was happening.

Friday,
October 4, 1918

Alan spent the night in Western Maryland Hospital, sleeping in the chair beside Emily's bed. Sitting in a wooden chair with a straight back wasn't the most-comfortable way to sleep and he woke up many times during the night. Each time he did, he would check on Emily to make sure she was still alive. He'd watch the rise and fall of her chest and listen for any tell-tale sign of her struggling to breathe. Other times he woke up in a panic because he heard Emily cough or moan.

Alan eventually woke up and saw daylight coming through the window and decided to give up sleeping altogether. Besides, his neck was stiff and his arms were numb from slumping in the wooden chair for so many hours.

It felt reminiscent of how he had sat beside Anne's bed. He prayed that it wouldn't end the same. He checked Emily again just to make sure that she was only sleeping.

Alan left her sleeping because she needed the rest. She had had a worse night than Alan with all her coughing and moaning. He walked out into the hall and blinked in the sudden light.

"You look a fright, Dr. Keener," Harriet Dinning said.

"Thank you, Harriet. I only hope that I am able to return the compliment someday."

Harriet smiled. "Not if I'm lucky. Why don't you go home and shower and change? Your wife will be fine here. She's finally getting some sleep. That will do her more good than anything. I'll keep a close watch on her for you."

Alan sighed and nodded. "I know you will."

Emily wouldn't miss him while she was sleeping and he couldn't do anything to help her. "I think that is a good idea. Thank you."

He walked outside to the car and drove home, all the while trying to ease the cramps from his neck as he did. Back in his house, the shower

84

felt good and helped refresh him. When he had dressed, he cooked himself some toast and eggs for breakfast. He was too nervous to handle the fried eggs in his stomach and only wound up nibbling on the piece of toast.

He detoured on his way back to the hospital to stop at a florist. He went inside and bought a nice arrangement of bright flowers that he hoped would brighten Emily's day. She loved flowers and grew many different varieties in her garden. He needed to do what he could to keep her stress from building to the point it had last night.

As Alan started to pass the money over to the florist, he realized that such a simple contact could be enough to spread the flu virus. He pulled his hand back quickly.

"Is something wrong, sir?" the florist asked. The man looked expectantly at the bills in Alan's hand.

Alan shook his head. He laid the money on the counter.

"No, I was just thinking about something else," Alan said.

As he walked out of the store, he wondered how many people were passing the virus back and forth between each other. It couldn't be stopped. The flu could be transmitted so easily, through air, by touch. It might even linger on things that a person had touched, waiting to jump to a non-infected person.

He stopped on the sidewalk outside of the florist and unconsciously wiped his hand on his coat. He wished he had soap and water nearby. He would scrub his hands raw just to be sure.

When Alan got back to the hospital, he found a note in his mailbox asking him to see Dr. Hyatt immediately. The doctor was in his office when Alan arrived.

"Doctor, come in. There are some things I need to tell you," Dr. Hyatt said when he saw Alan.

Hyatt wasn't frowning so Alan didn't think he was in trouble, but Hyatt wasn't smiling either. Not that it mattered. Hyatt didn't intimidate Alan any longer. They had reached a truce. Alan walked into the office and sat down in the chair.

Hyatt rubbed his eyes. "I'll get right to the point. The Board of Health considered your data and issued a health warning that should run this afternoon in the newspaper."

Alan tried to keep from smiling because Hyatt would take it the wrong way. "That's good."

Hyatt nearly fell into his chair. "Perhaps. We're not sure how much it will help, but if it keeps one person from getting sick, it will be worth it. We're trying to keep public gatherings of people to a minimum so as to not give the Spanish Flu a chance to spread easily. As such, the hospital will not be accepting any flu cases from this point forward."

"What are you talking about? This is a hospital. How can you turn away anyone who needs help?"

"Doctor, if this flu takes on even half of the scale that it has in other places, we aren't going to be able to help the people we need to help in this city. We had to draw the line somewhere to try and minimize infections. Some of the people are the most susceptible to the flu are here or at Allegany Hospital. We can't expose them to that risk."

"And what about the people with the flu who need our help?"

"Let's be honest, doctor, if someone has the flu, what can we do for him? At least here. The doctors will still visit patients in their homes. That won't change. They just won't be bringing them to the hospitals. It increases the opportunity for the flu to spread."

"So you're willing to let some people die?" Alan snapped.

Dr. Hyatt held up his finger. "Number one, I don't know that anyone I don't admit to this hospital will die. Most people survive the flu even this flu." He held up a second finger. "Number two, my duty here is not to a single patient but to everyone in this hospital. I am making a choice that I hope will allow the patients already here to get healthy."

Alan shook his head. "It's not right."

"The Board of Health could have quite easily added hospitals to its order and banned all cases from the hospitals. We chose a different route. We want to help who we can, but we can't help everyone. We must be cautious or we will only add to the problem. What we are hearing from around the country is that confined places like military camps, theaters and hospitals are fertile breeding grounds for the flu."

"Then we're giving up the battle as lost before we've even tried to find a way out."

Hyatt shrugged. "Doctor…Alan, if you can find a way to fight this, then I will support you. Until that time, we are making a strategic retreat in the face of a very deadly enemy. You did well by forcing the Board of Health to act, but now we've done what we can and I don't think it will be enough."

"Why not?"

"Eight people in this city died last night. All of them died from the flu." And one of them had been Anne. "We have an epidemic. We

86

can't stop it right now. We can only hope to slow it down."

Alan saw the Board of Health notice on page nine as he read the *Cumberland Evening Times*. He would have expected something so important to be placed closer to the front of the newspaper, but news of the war dominated the front pages. It was obviously winding down and people read the newspaper eagerly hoping for word of a signed treaty. Bulgaria had already signed the armistice a week ago.

Alan was just happy to see something in the newspaper. The Board of Health had considered the information Alan had supplied it and they had acted finally.

The three-paragraph order read like the actions many other communities had taken in the past few weeks. It recognized the problem and one of the ways the disease the transmitted. The final paragraph took the action.

"It is the order of the Board of Health of the City of Cumberland, that from this day, October 4, 1918, all schools, private and public, all churches and Sunday schools, theatres, public and private dance halls, and other places of indoor public assemblages (not including outdoor meetings) in the City of Cumberland, shall be closed and remain closed until this order is rescinded, of which time all persons interested shall have due and timely notice, and it is further ordered that all street cars or other public conveyances used or operated in the City of Cumberland shall keep all windows opened while in operation, until further notice and all persons are ordered to refrain from spitting on sidewalks, or other places, and are further requested to use their handkerchiefs when coughing or sneezing." Ralph Rizer, secretary pro-tem, signed the order.

Alan read it again and slowly shook his head.

It might help, but then again, similar precautions hadn't seemed to help much yet in other cities, though who is to say how bad things might had been if they hadn't taken precautions.

Alan walked into Emily's room. She was sitting up in bed and looking well rested. The circles under her eyes were gone and her hair had been brushed. She was reading her own copy of the newspaper. She laid it on her lap when she saw Alan.

"Are you going to let me go home?" she asked.

Alan smiled. "Tomorrow morning. I want you to get another good night of sleep."

Emily slapped her hands on the bed. "How can I sleep, knowing Anne is lying in that funeral home all alone?"

"You slept last night."

"That was exhaustion. Besides, have you read the paper? The entire city is being shut down because of this flu."

Alan nodded, but he didn't say anything.

"Will what the Board of Health wants to do work? Will it be enough to stop this thing that killed Anne from spreading?"

Alan slowly shook his head. "I don't think so. No one is sure what it will take to stop it. Did you see the article that said one-thousand men on the B&O had the flu? There's just no way to stop it unless you don't breathe and if you aren't breathing, you have some bigger problems to be worried about."

With one-sixth of its Cumberland work force sick with the flu, the railroad had brought in men from Baltimore and Philadelphia. Both were places harder hit with the flu than Cumberland. Alan had seen the notice and worried that some of these men, happy as they might be to get away from the devastation and death in their home cities, could very easily be bringing more flu to this area.

Cow saw the woman sitting on the park bench slumped over. He stopped walking and waited, watching the woman. He was afraid that she would be dead as Jared Scell had been when Cow had found him. He had no desire to see someone who had died from the Spanish Flu ever again.

Then Cow heard the woman cough. It was a sound so heavy with fluid that she may as well have been spitting.

He froze in mid-step.

A cough or spitting was as good as a bullet nowadays. Signs had gone up around town reading "Spitting equals death." The girl might be alive but for how much longer? Did she have the flu?

Cow had read the Board of Health warning in the newspaper. He knew that it had warned people to cover their mouths with a handkerchief when they coughed to keep the flu from spreading. This woman wasn't doing that. Her hands held onto the edge of the bench, almost as if to hold her body upright. She looked like she could barely raise her hand let alone cover her mouth. If she tried, she might fall off the bench.

Flu or not, she was sick and needed help. Cow stepped forward.

"Ma'am?" he said quietly. He didn't want to startle her.

The woman looked up and Cow recognized her. She was Lorene Sears. She had been two years behind him at Allegany County High School. She had been a friend of Cow's sister.

"Calvin?"

"What are you doing out on the street, Lorene?" he asked as he hurried to her side, completely forgetting the flu. "It's really not safe here."

That was no lie either. People were staying in their homes away from others. No one wanted to meet up with someone who might have the flu.

"Robert died in the army camp and I want to die with him," Lorene said.

Cow sat down next to her on the bench. Though he was worried about her, he was still careful not to touch her. He wasn't sure how easily Spanish Flu could jump from one person to another.

Cow had no idea who Robert was, but he obviously meant something to Lorene. Robert was probably her boyfriend.

"That's foolish talk," Cow said.

She shook her head and sobbed. "It's true. It's true. I don't want to live without him. We were going to be married and start a family. Now it's gone. It's all gone."

"Would Robert want you to do that?"

Lorene sniffled. "I don't know."

"Yes, you do. Look at how you're reacting to Robert dying. I have to think he wouldn't be acting the same if you had been the one who died."

Lorene shrugged. "It doesn't matter now. God is going to kill me. It's just a matter of time. I'm not one of his chosen ones."

Cow sighed. He had seen enough death from this flu already. He couldn't believe that this was anything God wanted.

"Not if I can help it," he muttered.

He stood up and jogged to a police call box. He used his box key to open the locked case. Inside was a telephone. Cow picked up the receiver and asked the operator to patch him through to a hospital.

When a nurse at Western Maryland Hospital answered, Cow said, "This is Patrolman Lewis. I'm on Greene Street near Riverside Park. I need an ambulance over here to pick up a sick person."

"I'll contact one of the funeral homes, but they've been pretty overworked lately." The funeral home hearses doubled as hospital ambulances in the city. "I'll send an ambulance over as soon as one is available," the nurse said.

Cow looked over at Lorene. She was slumped forward as if she was going to tumble off of the bench and onto the ground. Maybe she could wait. *Maybe.* The one thing he knew was that she needed help now.

"I don't think I can wait. I'll take care of it," Cow said.

He hung up and then placed a call to the station. "I need a car out on Greene Street by the park," he told the desk sergeant.

"I'll send someone out in a few minutes."

"Make it quick. This is an emergency."

With only four cars and twenty-nine officers, motorized patrols on the Cumberland Police Department were generally reserved for emergencies. While this certainly qualified, so did the other deathly ill cases in the city and there were plenty of those right now.

The black patrol car showed up in three minutes with Adam Hauser driving. Cow waved his arms so Adam would see him. The car stopped in front of Cow. He hurried around to the driver's side.

"What's the problem?" Adam asked.

"I've got a sick woman here who needs to get to the hospital."

"You pulled me over here for a sick woman?"

Cow nodded. "Yes. She needs help now."

"Has she got the flu?"

"What do I look like, a doctor? I don't know if she's got the flu but it looks like it," Cow snapped.

Adam's eyes widened. "I'm not taking her in this car. It's not an ambulance. Call the hospital and ask for help."

"I did. The ambulances are out and she needs help now. If you won't help her, then get out and I'll drive her in," Cow said.

"But I signed out this car."

"Then you drive her," Cow nearly yelled.

Adam frowned and climbed out of the car. Cow hurried over to the park bench where Lorene sat slumped over.

"Lorene, you need to go to the hospital," Cow said.

Lorene shook her head. "No, it won't do any good."

"It will. I've got a police car ready to drive you over."

Lorene shook her head once more.

Cow hesitated and then reached out and touched her on the shoulder. "Lorene."

She murmured something unintelligible and her eyes did not open. She tumbled forward, almost as if Cow's light touch had knocked her off balance.

Cow instinctively reached out and caught her. Now he had no choice. If he was trying to avoid catching the flu, it was too late.

Cow slid his arms under Lorene's shoulders and knees and carried her back to the car. He helped Lorene into the back seat while Adam backed away from the car. Cow looked at Adam and rolled his eyes. Then he slipped into the driver's seat.

"I'll take the car back to the station when I'm finished at the hospital," Cow said to Adam.

Traffic wasn't heavy this evening so Cow didn't need to use his siren. He turned onto Baltimore Street and sped down the hall and across the Western Maryland Railway, and moments later, the B&O Railroad tracks.

"Sorry," he said to Lorene when the car bounced hard as it hit the tracks.

Lorene didn't say anything. She was slumped across the back seat of the car. Cow wondered if she was even conscious. He prayed she wasn't dead.

Cow stopped the car in front of the Western Maryland Hospital. He climbed out of the car and helped Lorene out of the back. He started to walk her into the hospital but her knees buckled and she collapsed onto the street. Cow scooped her up once again and carried her through the front door.

The nurse on duty at the reception desk stood up when Cow hurried inside. Cow recognized her as a young nurse named Harriet Dinning.

"What's wrong, Cow?" she asked.

"This is Lorene Sears. I found her at Riverside Park. I think she's got the flu."

The nurse backed away. Cow stepped forward.

"No, Cow, keep her away," Harriet said.

"What are you talking about? She's sick. She needs help."

"We can't do anything for her."

Cow's eyes narrowed. "What? This is a hospital. You have a lot of doctors here. Certainly they can do something for her," Cow said loudly.

The nurse shook her head. "They can't stop it. This is beyond us."

"Then what good are you? Would you rather I take her back to Riverside Park and just let her die?" Cow nearly shouted.

He was not going to let Lorene die. He didn't want to see another Jared Scell. Even now, he could see her face in Scell's place as he lay dead on his bed, his body twisted in agony as he had died. Cow wasn't going to let that happen to Lorene. She had been kind to him in high school when everyone else had thought he was just a cow. He was going to show her that her kindness toward him hadn't been wasted.

"You are going to get a gurney," Cow said sternly. "Then you are going to admit this woman into the hospital and take care of her like you are supposed to do."

"You can't bully me, Cow," Harriet said. "We are not admitting any flu patients. The best place for them is home in their beds."

Down the hall, a door opened and Alan Keener stepped out. He saw the confrontation and walked over to Cow and the nurse.

"What's going on here that you both need to yell at each other?" Alan said.

"I'm trying to admit a patient, but the nurse won't let me," Cow said.

Alan looked at the nurse. "What's the problem?"

The nurse looked nervous. "You know what Dr. Hyatt said about flu cases, doctor."

Alan nodded. "But we are a hospital. We have a duty to perform. If we do not receive the sick and give them our best care, why are we here?"

"But we can't help her," the nurse insisted.

"We can't help many people we treat, but we make the effort because we must as healers," Alan said calmly.

"What of the other patients? The flu may spread."

"We will do our best to help them, too, but do I have the right to say who will live and who will die? I don't think so. I will help them all and leave the decision of life to the good Lord. Do we have any single rooms available?"

Harriet nodded. "Room twelve."

Alan nodded and motioned to Cow. "Follow me, Cow."

"Thanks, Doc."

"I don't know what we can do for her, Cow. The nurse wasn't lying about that. If this woman has the flu, we can only treat the symptoms and hope her body can take care of itself. No one has found anything that works against the flu yet."

Cow nodded. "Whatever you can do here is better than she was getting where I found her."

Alan held a door to a hospital room open. Cow stepped inside and laid Lorene on the bed. He started to pull off her shoes to make her more comfortable, but Alan put a hand on his arm.

"One of the nurses will take care of her," he said gently.

Cow stepped back and stared at Lorene. She looked so pale that she almost seemed to glow in the dim light of the room.

"What is happening to the world, Doc?" Cow asked.

Alan shrugged. "I wish I knew. It's almost like nature is trying to show us that she's still more powerful than man. No matter how many of each other we kill in war, nature can still kill more of us. No matter how much we think we know about life, she still can make us look impotent."

Cow didn't like the sound of desperation in Alan's voice. It scared him because he thought the doctors would be able to fix this mess.

"Will everyone die?" Cow asked.

Alan shook his head. "No, this flu is very contagious and very deadly, but that is compared to other flus. Indications I'm reading about are that about forty percent of the population will get the flu. More in some places than others. I'm hoping that since this is a fairly rural area, it won't be as much."

Cow did a quick calculation for how many people were in Cumberland and how many would get sick with the flu. Nearly ten thousand. It would be nearly impossible to walk down the street and not see someone who was sick.

He let out a long breath. "That's still a lot of people."

"Yes, it is, but only about two to three percent of those who get the flu will die. That's many times deadlier than the typical flu, but it is relatively low. The problem is that so many people will get the flu that the death rate will be large."

"What can I do to keep from getting it?" Cow asked.

Alan shrugged. "Pray. I can't help you. Only God will be able to."

Kolas stood under the light from a street lamp as the sun set over the Haystack Mountain. He looked out over the small crowd that had gathered around him to hear how they could live. He held up the newspaper over his head.

"Now you see the wrath of God begin to make itself known among the people. There is no stopping God or his chosen ones. The doctors can do nothing to prevent its spread. Even now, the evil, the foul, the failed among you begin to die. There is no place of safety in this war. Either you will serve God as an instrument of destruction or you will be destroyed."

"We go to church. We pray. What more can we do?" someone in the crowd called.

Kolas gave a sharp laugh. "That is not service to God. That is worship. Now God calls on his faithful to serve as his instruments to bring his wrath to the unfaithful. You must now act or be swept aside."

"How do we do that?" a woman asked.

"Take upon yourselves the sign of God. It will protect you from the avenging angels who cover this world just as the blood on the doors to their homes marked the Jews and kept them safe from the death that found the Egyptians. The sign of God will mark you to be tested as faithful. If you pass the test, as I did, then you will become a tool for your God to strike down the unbelievers."

One middle-aged man stepped forward and said, "I want to live."

"Will you serve if you are given life?" Kolas asked.

The man hesitated. "I think I'd do anything to avoid dying like my brother did yesterday. It was horrible. He couldn't breathe."

Kolas nodded. He licked his thumb, leaned forward and drew a cross on the man's forehead.

"Now, go. Return in four days ready to serve."

"Why that long?" the man asked.

"By then, the test will have been made. If you are still alive, you will have been prepared to serve," Kolas told him. "God's wrath will not be halted."

SATURDAY, OCTOBER 5, 1918

Alan walked into Emily's hospital room and saw the bed was empty. Where was his wife? She hadn't been released from the hospital yet. Alan was Emily's doctor and he hadn't authorized it. Then her head appeared behind a changing screen. She was dressing. Alan closed the door behind him.

"What are you doing?" he asked.

"It's Saturday. Anne's funeral is today. I'm getting ready," Emily told him.

Alan took a deep breath to prepare himself for an argument.

"You're sick, Emily," he said.

"I am not. I was just tired from everything that happened."

She walked around from behind the screen. She was wearing the black dress she had been wearing at the viewing when she collapsed.

"I'm fine, Alan."

She didn't look fine. She looked pale and slightly wobbly on her feet. Emily was still ill, no matter what she thought.

"Emily, I know you want to go to the funeral, but look at you. You're nearly ready to fall over now," Alan told her.

She walked across the room and put a hand on his cheek. "Darling, you're my doctor. You can sign me out."

Alan was torn between allowing her to say goodbye to Anne or protecting Emily and their unborn child. He kept seeing Emily collapse at the funeral parlor. The fall played itself over and over in his mind. He saw her fall in slow motion. He heard the thud as she hit the floor, but most of all, he felt his fear. He couldn't allow that to happen again. He had lost his parents and brother because of the war. He had lost his daughter to the flu. He couldn't stand to lose his wife and unborn child to the flu as well. It was too much to ask of him.

Alan shook his head. "I can't, Emily. I can't. You're sick. I don't

95

want you to get worse. Anne wouldn't want that."

Emily sobbed. She leaned against the side of the bed and punched at it with her fist. He ran toward her, but she pushed him away. Alan reluctantly backed off a step.

"Emily, I can't let you go. The baby could have been killed when you collapsed at the viewing. You have to consider that. Would Anne want her baby brother or sister hurt?"

"What kind of mother would I be if I didn't attend my own daughter's funeral? This is the last thing I will be able to do as Anne's mother. After today, she's gone forever."

"It also might be the last thing you do as the baby's mother," Alan countered.

Alan moved forward and helped Emily back into her bed. She resisted slightly, but she wasn't even strong enough to push him away. She could not have lasted through the funeral service.

"What kind of mother am I to do this?" Emily asked.

A good one who cares about her baby."

He leaned over and kissed her on the cheek. He could taste her slightly salty tears. It broke his heart to be keeping her in the hospital, but he had to look at things as a doctor and not as a husband.

Alan sat with her for half an hour until she fell asleep. Then he quietly crept out of the room. He walked down Baltimore Street and then headed for the funeral home.

Alan arrived early at the Louis Stein Funeral Home so that he could say goodbye to his daughter before the casket was closed and she was sealed away forever. Then she would be taken to St. Patrick's and be lost to him forever.

It still seemed unreal to him. Last week at this time, Anne had been playing with an imaginary friend named Jasper and hosting a tea party for her dolls.

At the funeral home, Louis Stein saw Alan walk inside. Louis stood up and walked out of his office near the front of the house. He was wearing a black suit and Alan tried to remember if he had ever seen him wearing anything else.

"Dr. Keener," Stein said, holding out his hand.

Alan stopped and shook Stein's hand. "I came to see my daughter."

Stein nodded. "So I guessed. There are a few details about the service I need to speak with you about. Would you come into my office, please?" He stepped aside to allow Alan into the office.

Alan sat down at one of the chairs in front of the large oak desk. Stein sat down and lifted a copy of the *Cumberland Evening Times* from the center of the desk.

"You've read yesterday's newspaper?" Stein asked.

Alan eyes narrowed. Stein was going to make a point with the paper and Alan wondered if he had missed something.

"Yes, I have."

"The Board of Health order has forced some changes to the funeral."

Alan cocked his head to the side. "What sort of changes?"

"We can't have the service at St. Patrick's or the final viewing here. They are considered public gatherings and hence, prohibited from the order."

Alan closed his eyes and tried not to cry. The Spanish Flu had not only taken his daughter from him, it wouldn't let him say goodbye to her.

He said, "I understand. We'll just have a graveside service. Open-air services are still allowed."

Stein's shoulders sagged and he lowered his head. Slowly he shook his head "no."

"We can do that, but we don't have a grave," Stein said slowly.

"What?"

"Rose Hill is falling behind in its grave digging. The flu has taken its toll on their workers at the same time the demand for their services has increased. They, and most of the other cemeteries in town, can't keep up with the need for new graves."

Alan put his hand over his face and slumped in the chair. As if it wasn't bad enough that he had lost his daughter, now he couldn't put her to rest. What kind of killer was this that would kill children and then not let them be buried? The world was going crazy!

"When can she be buried?" Alan asked.

Stein looked at his calendar. "Monday morning at the earliest and that would only be if no more workers catch the flu. I believe we could safely hold the service in the early afternoon Monday. I can make the appropriate calls and get the notice in the newspaper for you."

Alan nodded numbly.

It frightened him that so many people were dying. It meant that the Board of Health warning had come too late. The flu had already spread wildly throughout the city and was now beginning to make itself known. Now it was simply killing many of those people it had already infected before the Board of Health had taken action.

How had it spread so easily? It seemed as if it was infecting everyone at once. What was so different about the Spanish Flu from other forms of influenza?

What was it Lorene Sears had said that street preacher Kolas had talked about...the wrath of God was upon the world? Maybe he was right. A world war and a flu pandemic at the same time. If that wasn't God's wrath, Alan didn't know what was.

Louis stood up and patted Alan on the shoulder. Alan simply sat on the chair and stared out the window. He couldn't see his daughter. He couldn't say goodbye to her. Tears rolled down his cheeks.

Alan left the funeral home and walked over to St. Patrick's Church, just a block away. A notice on the door to the church announced that Mass could no longer be held indoors but Father Wunder would be holding outdoor Mass in the yard in front of the St. Patrick's Church weather permitting. Spanish Flu had even driven God from his sanctuary.

Alan walked to the side of the church to the brick house that served as the rectory. He knocked on the door and Father Wunder answered it.

"Hello, Alan," the priest said. "How are you? I'm sorry about the changes to the funeral plans for Anne. I'm sure you don't need that type of stress in your life right now. I heard that Emily was ill and in the hospital. How is she?"

"Right now, she's resting in the hospital, but her health is fragile."

"I will say a prayer for her and light a candle on her behalf."

"Thank you, Father. I understand about the funeral changes. After all, I was the one who was pushing for the Board of Health to do something about the flu. How can I argue that it inconveniences me when they took the action I wanted?"

"Mr. Stein just called me a few moments ago to reschedule the service for Monday afternoon at the graveside."

Alan nodded. "I just left there."

"Yes, he told me. That's why I'm a bit surprised to see you here. I would think you would have gone home."

"I needed to talk to you."

Father Wunder stepped back and opened the door wider so that Alan could walk inside.

"Then come in and we'll sit down. Would you like some tea?"

Alan shook his head.

Alan sat down on the end of the couch near the fireplace. He stared at the logs laying in the hearth ready to be lit. What was it that he had learned in college? No matter is ever lost. It only changes form and state. A log might burn in a fire, but the matter still remained in the form of ash and debris in the smoke the burning log gave off.

Did that hold true for Anne? Would she take another form? Would she still be Anne even if she were in another form?

Father Wunder sat down in an armchair near the door. He took off his reading glasses and lit a pipe. Then he stayed into Alan's eyes.

"What is troubling you, Alan?" Father Wunder asked.

"I find myself thinking about death almost all the time lately," Alan admitted.

"That's understandable given the circumstances."

Alan hesitated and then said quickly, "I'm scared."

"There's no use being scared of something that is unavoidable. Death is part of life. If we accept one, we must accept the other."

"But so many people will be taken before their time because of the flu. Some already have been. Anne was."

Father Wunder shook his head causing the smoke from his pipe to curl around his head. "How do you know they will be taken from this world before their time? You can't say that. Only God knows the time of a person's death."

Alan grinned slightly. "That's a horrible thing to tell a doctor, Father."

Father Wunder returned the grin. "Would you have me lie?"

Alan shook his head.

"Besides you know all of this already. Why does it scare you now?" Father Wunder asked.

Alan stood up and began pacing the room. "Because this time I know I have no control over any of it. I watched my daughter die in front of me. She withered away like a cut flower in the heat. Now there is this hole in my life that I don't know if I can ever fill."

"Is control over life so important to you?"

"Not just to me, but to any doctor. We're supposed to have the answers to keep people healthy. If we don't have those answers, why should people come to us for help? If we can't protect people from something as common as the flu, then what good are we? We're kidding ourselves that we're doing any good." Alan stopped and leaned against the fireplace mantle and was surprised to find he was breathing hard.

Father Wunder nodded slowly. "I can't tell you how to fight the

Spanish Flu, other than to do the best that you can. Never give up in your search for an answer. That is how all of the progress medicine has made has been achieved. Men have sought answers to life's mysteries until they were found. You face such a mystery now. You are God's tool in this work. While he will take no one before his time, you are his instrument to save those he wishes to be saved from the flu in this community and others."

"Kolas thinks differently."

Father Wunder's brow wrinkled. "Kolas?"

"He's a street preacher who is telling everyone who will listen to him that God wants the flu to spread through Cumberland, through Allegany County, throughout the world. He says God wants people to die and Kolas is the instrument in God's hand to spread the flu."

Father Wunder rubbed his temples. "I hate to speak against another man of God, but it does not sound as if this man Kolas is a man of God. God is love. He is our father in heaven. He loves each of us. He loves you. He loves Anne. When we die, he grieves as a father would grieve, as you did over Anne. Did God not give Noah a sign after the flood that he would not wipe out mankind as he did during the flood?"

Alan nodded. "He did, but then how do you explain this pandemic that is certainly trying to kill all of mankind?"

"I can't. I can tell you, though, that it is his will that this happen or it would not be happening. It is not being done out of anger, however."

"The result is still the same. People are dying."

Father Wunder held up a cautionary finger. "No, I don't think the results are the same. To know that you may die because it is God's will or that you may die because God is angry with you or that you may die as a simple quirk of fate all have different meanings."

"You're still just as dead," Alan said.

Father Wunder paused and took a deep breath. "No man knows his time upon this earth. Because of this, the thing for each of us to do is to live our lives as if each day was the last day of our lives. We should live to please God. Take nothing for granted. Do not miss putting off needed change. Then when the day comes that you die, you will know it is not because God is angry at you but that he thinks you have been a faithful enough servant that he wants to meet you."

"Medical research has the ability to delay death, though, so children like Anne have a chance to live," Alan countered.

Father Wunder took his pipe from his mouth and pointed the shank at Alan. "Really? Then why couldn't medical research save your daughter from the flu?"

Alan looked away and shrugged. He didn't have an answer. He had failed Anne. This flu was nothing like other forms of the flu. It wasn't even attacking the same people. The common flu generally killed the very young and very old. Spanish Flu was not only killing those people but also twenty to forty-five year olds.

Father Wunder cocked his head to the side and raised his eyebrows. "Then consider the possibility that maybe it was Anne's time to die. Maybe she didn't need to live a full life to be ready to return to God's embrace. Maybe she was too good for this world."

"But if I had known the cure…"

Father Wunder stood up and put an arm on Alan's shoulder. "Do you really think you can thwart God's plan?"

The words sunk in and Alan realized that he couldn't. He had no power over death.

"I can't believe it is God's plan that so many people die," he said.

"Why not? Life and death are inextricably linked. For you or anyone to try and change that seems arrogant to me. If man's control over death is so great, why is there not a cure for this modern plague? From what I have read, this bout of influenza is different in many ways than the typical influenza. That does not seem like a random act to me. When it is time…when the goals of God have been accomplished, then the flu will be controlled. Not until then."

Cow walked along Mechanic Street, enjoying the crisp fall air. He saw Jack Montgomery walking along the street toward him.

"Good afternoon, Jack," Cow said.

Jack barely glanced at him. He waved and then covered his mouth and nose with his coat as he hurried to the other side of the street.

Things like that had been happening a lot lately. People were scared. This flu was a hidden killer. No one knew how to avoid it or if it was coming for them. Everyone walked around with a guarded look on their faces and their nerves taut. It was as if they expected the flu to be a thug hidden in the shadows of an alley.

Cow walked by the Mechanic Street Saloon and saw movement inside. He sighed and stepped through the door. He knew what was going to happen. He could almost recite all of the lines that would be said because he had gone through the same scene four times already today.

What surprised him was that this bar was on one of the main streets of the city. The bars that were trying to stay open despite the Board of Health order were generally the neighborhood bars off the beaten path so they didn't attract attention from police officers like Cow.

The barroom was dim inside. Two-thirds of the lamps had been turned off to make it harder to see anything that was going on inside. That told Cow that this bar wasn't accidentally open because the owner hadn't read the Board of Health notice.

Half a dozen people nuzzled beers and other drinks; two men sat at the bar and three men and a woman sat at the tables. When people were afraid, they sought solace in the arms of alcohol. Then for a few hours, they could forget what was happening outside of the saloon. In this case, unfortunately, that solace would last until the flu struck inside the bar.

"I'm sorry to do this everyone, but this bar has to close down," Cow announced loudly.

Tom Jenkins, the owner and the bartender, threw his bar towel down. "What are you talking about Cow? We've got a license to serve."

"I'm not talking about liquor licenses. I'm talking about trying to keep you all alive. The Board of Health added pool rooms and bars to the businesses, licensed or not, that have to close down until further notice," Cow explained.

Tom threw his hands up in the air. "C'mon, Cow. There's no flu in here."

Cow shrugged. "I'm not a doctor. I wouldn't know if the flu is here or not and neither would you. I do know that if the flu does get in here, it will move through everyone pretty quickly. You won't be able to stop it once it starts."

Tom shuddered. "How long do I have to stay closed down?"

"Until the Board of Health lifts the order, which will probably be when the flu season is over," Cow told him.

"Flu season's not over until months from now! Staying closed that long will put me out of business! That's un-American!"

Cow walked up to the bar, leaned across it and said very slowly, "Would you rather die from Spanish Flu? How patriotic is that?"

"You don't know that will happen!" Tom yelled, slapping his hands on the bar.

Cow held his ground. He hadn't backed down when they other bartenders had yelled and he wouldn't back down from Tom Jenkins.

"You don't know that it won't. Besides, it doesn't matter what you think. The Board of Health has the authority to close businesses during a crisis and that's what they are doing. It's the law and if you want to keep your license, you'll obey it."

Tom waved a finger in Cow's face. "This is not right! It's not right."

From his tone, Cow could tell Tom had given in. He wouldn't fight being closed any longer.

Cow turned his attention to the crowd. "Okay, everyone listen up. This bar and any bars in the city are closed until further notice. You have to leave...now."

Most of the people stood up and slowly walked out, though they grumbled. They buttoned their overcoats tightly up to their necks and pulled their hats down low over their ears. Then they slunk out into the overcast day. Some of the people bought a bottle of liquor on their way out. Cow waited and watched them leave, ignoring the mean glares some of the people shot his way.

Finally, only Cow, Tom and a single man sitting at the bar were left inside. The man hadn't made any move to leave. He leaned over the bar and quietly sipped his drink.

"It's time to go, sir," Cow said.

"I'm not ready to leave," the man snapped.

He turned away from Cow and clutched his drink tightly between his hands.

Cow sighed. Someone always had to make his job difficult.

"I think you are finished," Cow said.

The man tilted his head back and swallowed the rest of his drink. Cow wondered how many he had had tonight.

"Tommy, I want another drink," the man growled.

The man banged his glass against the bar. Tom moved to refill the glass. Cow held up his hand and waved Tom away.

"Don't do it unless you want wind up in jail," Cow warned him.

"For serving him a drink?" Tom asked.

"For breaking the law. We just went through that," Cow said sternly.

Tom sighed and backed away. The man looked around, angry.

"What gives? What's a man have to do to get a drink anymore?"

"It's time to leave," Cow repeated.

The man threw his glass at Cow. Cow swayed to the side and glass shattered against the wall behind him. Cow stepped forward quickly and grabbed the man by his shirt. He yanked the man off the bar stool and brought him close to his face.

"Do you want to die, mister?" Cow asked.

The man laughed. "You won't kill me."

The man's alcoholic breath brought tears to Cow's eyes. He blinked them away.

"If I leave you here, you might catch the flu," Cow said.

The man snorted. "So what? I've had the flu before."

"Not this flu. If you catch the Spanish Flu, it will try to kill you. You won't be able to breathe because your lungs will fill with fluid. You'll burn up with fever. Your body will die in small pieces and you'll know it because patches of skin on your feet and face will begin to turn black. Not that you'll be aware of it. By that time, you'll be delirious if you're even conscious. When you finally die, it will be like drowning. You'll try to take a breath and you won't be able to breathe in because of the fluid in your lungs. You will die painfully, but you will have had your drinks."

The man paled. Cow turned slightly and pushed him toward the door.

"Is that what you want?" Cow asked.

"How do you know what will happen?" the man asked.

"How do you know it won't? I've seen it happen. I'm watching it happen now to other people."

The man stared at Cow for a moment. Then he shrugged and shuffled out of the bar without saying another word.

Cow looked over at Tom.

"His name is Chris Rydell," Tom said.

"Is he going to cause trouble?"

Tom shook his head. "No, he likes to drink and it makes him a little short tempered, but he's never gotten violent." Tom paused. "Cow, what you told him, was that the truth?"

"Yes."

Tom took a deep breath. "How do you stop something like that?"

"You don't. You just have to hope that you can avoid it and that means doing what the Board of Health feels strongly enough about to order. Make sure you're shut down when I come by again."

Cow walked out of the bar. He still had to look into other taverns that might be open illegally. Hopefully, he wouldn't run into as many hard heads as Chris Rydell. Cow would prefer not to remember how this flu killed.

As he walked down Mechanic Street, he noticed there weren't as many people on the street as typically were out and those that were kept a lot of space between themselves. The few people that were outside weren't talking and they barely even looked at each other. Those people were being cautious. Cow could understand that but it saddened him to see how scared the flu was making everyone. It was destroying the sense of community in the city.

Cow swung by Western Maryland Hospital during his rounds to check on Lorene. When he walked in the Baltimore Street doors, the first person he saw was Harriet, the nurse he had argued with to get Lorene admitted.

Cow took a deep breath and walked up to her. "Harriet, I'm sorry about threatening you last night. I should not have acted like that."

Harriet shook her head. "No need. I don't blame you."

"I was just worried about Lorene. I didn't want her to die."

"I understand, Cow. I might have done the same thing. I was just worried about keeping my job. I'm glad Dr. Keener stepped in."

"Can I go back to see Lorene?"

Harriet nodded. "She probably just finished up with her lunch."

Cow knocked on the door to Lorene's room. When there was no answer, he slowly pushed open the door. The room was dim because no lights were turned on, but he could see Lorene lying in the bed with her eyes open. He stared at her. She was so still that he wondered if she were dead.

"Lorene."

"Hello, Calvin," she said.

Her voice didn't sound too strong and he wondered how sick she was.

"Why didn't you answer my knock?"

"I don't want to see anyone."

"Why not? You look a lot better than you did last night." He stepped inside the room. "The nurse who told me your room number said that you were doing better. She thinks you only had a mild case of the flu. You should be happy. You'll live."

Lorene looked away from him. "I wanted to die, Calvin."

He sat down in the chair next to the bed. "You wanted to die? Why? Why would you want to do something like that?"

"I was in love, Calvin. Have you ever been in love?"

He shrugged. "Yes, but it only went one way."

"Well, that wasn't the way with Robert and me. We were going to get married. We were engaged. Then he got drafted into the army."

"The war is almost over they say. Robert will be home before you know it."

Lorene shook her head furiously. "No, no he won't, Calvin. The flu killed him."

Cow silently chided himself for sticking his foot in his mouth. "I'm sorry. Me and my big mouth."

"Don't blame yourself. It's not your fault. It's the flu."

"Wishing yourself dead won't bring Robert back, Lorene."

"I know, but I don't want to live without him. We were in love."

"Lots of soldiers are dying, Lorene. Their wives aren't trying to kill themselves."

"I'm not them!" Lorene snapped.

"No, you're not, but maybe you should consider that you're not supposed to die yet. The world is afraid of the flu. A lot of people are catching it and a lot of people are dying. You only had a mild case. I would say God is protecting you. You ought not to waste the life he's given you. Maybe there's a reason he still wants you around," Cow suggested.

"He didn't kill me with the flu, Calvin, because he'd already killed me by killing Robert."

Cow stared at her without saying anything. What could he say? Lorene had made up her mind to die. She simply lay on her bed, staring out the window at the passing cars on Baltimore Avenue.

To Cow, it seemed that the flu had found another way to kill. He stood up and left the room without even telling Lorene goodbye.

Sunday,
October 6, 1918

Alan held up the small beaker and stared at the cloudy fluid that covered the bottom of it. Could this be a cure to the Spanish Flu?

"Do you think it will really work?" Peter Markwood asked.

Alan shrugged. "I have no idea, but everyone seems to have hopes for this vaccine. It is what other physicians are experimenting with on their flu patients."

Peter shook his head. "I just don't know. Maybe we should wait and see what their results are before we test anyone with it. I'm not certain that it will work."

The fluid in the beaker was a potential vaccine against the flu. Alan and Peter had developed it from the research that some of the harder- and earlier-hit communities were doing into the Spanish Flu. It was a biological soup created from the body secretions of those with the flu. Peter had filtered the secretions to get rid of the large cells and other debris. It was an idea that had worked in the past to combat diphtheria and many doctors were hoping the theory would be as sound in combating the Spanish Flu.

"Do you think we can afford to wait? We've got twenty to thirty people dying each day in this county and ten times that number catching the flu," Alan said.

"No, I guess we have to try," Peter admitted, shaking his head. He frowned when he looked at the beaker and its contents.

"We've got a few patients with the flu in the hospital. With their permission, we'll test the vaccine on them. If we're lucky, we should see favorable results in a couple days."

"And if it doesn't work?"

Alan frowned. "Then the dying will continue and we'll look for something else."

Alan filled ten glass syringes with the vaccine. More vaccine was being filtered for additional doses. He took the first ten syringes. Peter would get the next ten that could be filled from the vaccine being filtered.

Alan headed out of the laboratory to the patients' rooms to test the vaccine. The first patient on Alan's list was Lorene Sears. Her room door was open when he arrived and he saw a man inside the room with Lorene. Alan stepped to the side and waited.

"You have survived and passed the test," the man said.

"So what does that mean, Kolas?" Lorene asked.

Kolas. So this was the street preacher who was teaching that the Spanish Flu was the wrath of God. He was the fool who wanted the flu to spread. What would such a man do to see that it happened?

"You have been chosen. You can now stand with me to be God's instrument in this battle to bring humility to humanity," Kolas told Lorene.

"But I wanted to die like you said that I would."

Kolas patted her shoulder. "I didn't say you would die. I said you would be tested and failing the test would mean death. You have not failed. You have been chosen to serve."

"How can I do that?"

"God has given you your life to work as his tool. Others must be tested as you and I have been. The worthy will live and those evil will die."

Alan rolled his eyes.

Kolas was dangerous. While the rest of the county was trying to find ways to prevent the spread of the flu, he was looking for ways to spread it and the more it spread, the more people would die.

Alan stepped into the doorway and pasted a smile on his face.

"Hello, Lorene. How are you feeling today?" he asked.

Startled, Kolas jumped and glared at Alan. Then he stepped to the side of the room. Alan moved to the side of the bed so he could still watch Kolas.

Lorene shrugged. "Better I suppose."

"I'm sorry to interrupt your visit, but I need to give you an injection."

"What kind of injection?" Kolas asked, nodding toward the syringe.

"A vaccine for the flu."

Kolas suddenly looked alarmed. He stared at Lorene as if expecting her to protest. Alan even expected her to protest. She just held her arm out.

"How do you know that is a vaccine?" Kolas asked.

"Do you think it's poison?" Alan snapped.

"No, of course not, but how do you know that it will vaccinate Lorene against the flu? I did not know there was a cure."

"Scientists and doctors around the world have been searching for a solution to the Spanish Flu. This is what they think will work."

"What if God does not want a solution found?"

"Then he's not the God I've been worshipping," Alan said.

Alan held up the syringe and knocked the air bubbles out of the tube by flicking his finger against it. He swabbed Lorene's arm with alcohol and then he injected the vaccine into her vein. She winced but she didn't cry out.

"There," Alan said. "Hopefully, this will get rid that flu. If it works, we may use it on everyone. You will be a tool to help God fight this flu."

He chose his words carefully to tweak Kolas. The street preacher scowled but didn't say anything. Too bad. Alan was hoping for an argument.

"It doesn't really matter," Lorene muttered.

"I wouldn't say that. Your friend Cow went to a lot of trouble to make sure you were taken care of when he brought you into the hospital. I think it would be the height of ingratitude if you died on him," Alan told her.

Alan smiled to let her know he was joking.

Lorene just stared at him. "Calvin is a nice person. I knew him in high school. He used to get picked on in school but he just took it because he didn't want to hurt anyone. He was too nice."

"You should be happy about that. His being nice saved your life."

"Like I said, he was too nice."

Monday,
October 7, 1918

Lorene rubbed the sore spot on her arm and looked out the window of her room. She still felt a little under the weather, but by and large, it was hard for her to call herself sick much less dead.

So had Dr. Keener's vaccine worked? She doubted that because she had already been feeling better when he had given her the vaccine yesterday. She felt that he had given it to her more as a precaution to make sure she continued to get well.

Too bad he couldn't give her a vaccine to heal her broken heart.

Was Kolas right then? Had God saved her so that she could help him spread the flu? She didn't want to hurt anyone else, but why was she still alive when so many others were dying from the flu? She was willing to die. Let her die and in trade, let someone who wants to live do so.

Kolas must be right. She only had a mild bout with the flu when so many others were dying from it. She had been tested as Kolas had said she would be and she had survived the test. Should she waste that opportunity now? Why had she been found worthy?

How could she serve God in the way Kolas talked about?

A tall nurse walked into the room with Lorene's breakfast of porridge and milk on a tray. She set the tray in front of Lorene.

"You look much better this morning, dear," the nurse said.

"I suppose."

"You don't sound happy about it. Don't you realize you could have died? This flu is scary, but you were one of the lucky ones."

Lorene nodded. "But what do I do now?"

The world was going crazy as people panicked over how to stop the Spanish Flu. Stores were closed. People were afraid to be together.

"The doctor said you can be released this morning," the nurse told Lorene.

"I guess you'll be glad to have me out of here."

The nurse paused. "No offense, but yes. We've got a third of our nurses out with the flu. That means there's more work for the rest of us and the hospital is filled to capacity even with the doctors trying to get the flu patients to stay home. I've been working all night and I'm ready to drop, but I have to wait until someone comes to work to replace me."

After the nurse left the room, Lorene ate her porridge and considered what the nurse had said. The hospitals were short staffed and needed help. She had heard yesterday from another nurse that the hospitals, especially the emergency hospitals, were looking for volunteers. In fact, that nurse had been a teacher who wasn't teaching right now because the Board of Health order had closed schools.

If Lorene volunteered to help as a nurse, she would be in a position to help Kolas in his mission to be the wrath of God. She wasn't sure exactly what she could do to spread the flu, but certainly she would have the opportunity. Kolas would have to tell her what he needed her to do to help him.

Kolas stood on a box in the middle of Riverside Park. More than fifty people stood around him. All of them looked to him for answers and guidance through this crisis. He was ready to show them the way to salvation by serving God's needs.

Kolas held his hands up and the crowd went silent. "Brothers and sisters, you can see around you the signs that God will not be thwarted.

"The doctors are confounded by what they call Spanish Influenza. But they know how to treat flu and flu does not kill. So this scourge can't be the flu. No matter how they change the name. What is it then?

"I will tell you what it is.

"It is God's wrath released upon the world.

"The politicians are scared people will vote them out office because they can't make them well. Dead people can't vote for them at all.

"The warmongers are humbled because God is striking more people dead than all the bullets and bombs combined.

"Just as God once destroyed the world by flood for the evil that existed then, so he will now do the same with the flu. Only this time, he has chosen to preserve his faithful not with an ark but with an immunity to this modern plague that is streaking through the population," Kolas preached.

111

"How can we serve him without risking catching the flu ourselves?" a woman asked.

"Do not fear the flu. You must demonstrate your faith and endure the fire. If your desire to serve God is true and your heart is pure, then you have nothing to fear, for the plague will pass you by."

Kolas pointed to Lorene who stood off to the side listening to him. She seemed to shrink under the attention that suddenly turned her way. Kolas waved her out from the crowd and over in front of him. Lorene walked toward him slowly. Her legs were still a bit shaky from her bout with the flu.

Kolas laid one hand on her shoulder and pointed his left hand at the crowd. "This woman has chosen to serve God. She faced the test with open eyes. The flu struck her but fled in the face of God's protection. Now she knows she has been chosen to serve as God's instrument to express his displeasure with mankind. Her faith is total now and she can go forth to serve his purpose unafraid. You must all choose now whom you will serve. To hesitate is to die," Kolas said.

"How?" a few people called.

"Come forward and take upon yourself the mark of God as Lorene did. This will prepare you for the test you will face and give you the strength to survive if you are true to God. Come now, before the plague takes you without the sign."

A line of people began to form in front of Kolas. He smiled and raised his hands into the air and looked into the sky.

"Thy will be done."

Alan plopped down in his chair at his desk. He laid his notes from his rounds in front of him. He had checked on all twenty people who had been given the vaccine for the flu. He had hoped that he would find a significant improvement in their conditions.

The vaccine had failed. He had seen no change in the patients. In fact, two of the worst cases had only continued to worsen and they died overnight. While it was true Lorene Sears had been released from the hospital, she had been on the mend anyway. She had just continued to improve. He couldn't take any credit for it. The vaccine hadn't accelerated her recovery.

Alan wadded up the papers and threw them into the wastebasket.

Worthless!

Days of work had been wasted. It was all worthless.

He had to find some way to fight the flu. Not everyone who caught the flu died. In fact, very few died, considering how deadly some diseases could be. Only about twenty-five people out of every thousand who caught the flu died. The problem was that one out of every two people seemed to catch the Spanish Flu. If he could reduce that number, it would reduce the number of people who died.

But it wouldn't save everyone.

It wouldn't save Sarah Jenkins. It wouldn't save Anne.

What was so different about the survivors that allowed them to survive the flu or not even catch it? Something in their blood, something in their bodies brought them safety. What was it?

Alan wished he could find people he knew were immune to the flu, but there was no way he could know that for sure. Someone he thought was immune simply might not have caught the flu yet.

He did know people who had survived the flu. He could compile a list of their names. If he could study the flu survivors and find their physical commonalities and compare those commonalities to people who had fallen victim to the flu, he might find a solution. The differences between the two groups could be the solution to fighting the flu.

Alan took out a sheet of paper from the drawer and wrote across the top, "Survivors." The first name he wrote was Lorene Sears.

Lorene walked up to the door of the house at 28 Washington Street. She noticed that all of the windows and transoms were cracked open, despite the day being cold. She paused to smooth out the wrinkles in her dress, closed her coat and then knocked on the door.

A young woman who looked only a few years older than Lorene answered the door and seemed relieved to see Lorene.

"Yes?" the woman asked.

"I heard that this house was being turned into an emergency hospital to treat people with the flu. I would like to help," Lorene explained.

The woman smiled. "We certainly can use the help. I was relieved to see you weren't a patient. Please come in."

When Lorene had asked about helping at Western Maryland Hospital, the nurse there had told her that the Red Cross was opening an emergency hospital on Washington Street and volunteers would be needed to help with the growing number of flu patients. Estimates now were that five thousand to six thousand people had the flu in Cumberland alone. Most of the sick stayed home, but severe cases — those

113

most likely to die — were being brought into the hospitals.

Inside the house, the front parlor had been cleared of home furnishings. Two desks and a number of plain, straight-back chairs had been set up. This was the receiving room for the new hospital.

"I'm Janet Coulson. The hospital superintendent is Mrs. Lichtenstein. She is upstairs right now setting up cots in the rooms that will serve as the wards. We're filling the rooms with as many as we can because so many people have the flu," said the young nurse.

Lorene shook Janet's hand and said, "I'm Lorene Sears. Can I get work here? The nurse at Western Maryland told me you needed volunteers."

"Aren't you afraid of catching the flu?"

Lorene shrugged. "Not really. I've had it and have gotten over it."

"You're lucky. My youngest brother died from it two days ago." Janet closed her eyes and shuddered as she recalled the experience. "Why don't you help me move some boxes of supplies into the basement? When Mrs. Lichtenstein comes down and sees you working, she'll probably hire you right away. We need the help as much as anyone else."

Lorene nodded and followed Janet to a back room where supplies from the Red Cross were stacked. The boxes were filled with syringes, bandages and bed linens. It didn't seem like enough supplies to run a hospital, even a small one.

"Is this all?" Lorene asked.

Janet snorted. "It's all we can get. I don't know how they expect us to help anyone if they don't send us the drugs and other medicines we ask for."

"Why don't they?"

"Because everybody else wants them, too, and there's not enough to go around."

"Then what can you do to help someone who's sick?"

Janet shrugged. "Keep them as comfortable as possible, I guess."

"So what do we do with these supplies?"

"We're going to need this space for a ward so our storage area and morgue will be downstairs where it's too damp for patients."

Morgue. So they were already expecting patients here to die.

Lorene took off her coat and laid it on a chair. Then she picked up a box and followed Janet toward the stairs. The basement was cool and damp. Unlike the plaster walls upstairs, these walls were rough stone. Half of it was filled with furniture, leaving very little storage space for the supply boxes.

When they came up from the basement, an older woman was standing in the supply room. She was counting the boxes and checking them off on a list.

"Who are you?" the woman asked when Lorene walked into the room.

"Lorene Sears. I was told you needed volunteers. I'd like to help," Lorene answered.

The woman lowered her list and smiled. "Do you have nursing experience?"

"No, but I'm willing to work and I'm not afraid of the flu."

The woman rolled her eyes. "Then you're foolish, girl. We're not adventurers here. We are caregivers."

"But I want to help," Lorene insisted.

"So did the other women who came here. Then they saw their first person killed by the flu and I never saw them again."

"I won't run."

"Ah, so you're tough. I had other tough nurses. They stayed and worked hard until they dropped from exhaustion. They were no good to me then. If you're looking to dare death, I don't want you," Mrs. Lichtenstein said.

That's exactly what Lorene wanted to do. She wanted to catch the flu — a good case this time — and die just like Robert had.

"I want to help, ma'am," Lorene said.

Lichtenstein looked her over and nodded. "Well we can use the help. I've got just enough staff to keep one nurse at each of the emergency hospitals. I can't afford to turn anyone away. Get back to work."

Lorene smiled and picked up another box.

Alan sat in a folding chair under a large tent in front of St. Patrick's. Father Wunder conducted an open-air mass, which did not violate the Board of Health's order.

Alan sat admiring the sunrise as it slowly lit up the morning sky. He watched the line of light creep across the ground chasing away the shadows. It was as if the mass was bringing a dawning of understanding to the world. How he wished it could be that simple.

The air was cool, but Alan simply kept his coat on as did everyone else. The cool air helped keep his thoughts clear. He wouldn't have missed the opportunity for anything. He only wished that Emily had come with him.

She had chosen to stay home, withdrawn and still upset over Anne's death. Alan hoped that she would work her way out of the depression soon because it certainly wasn't healthy for the baby she now carried. Emily needed a healthy attitude and spirit as well as a body free from Spanish Flu.

Emily needed to be here, listening to the words of God. Alan felt closer to God than he ever had before as sat under the roof of God's creation. He could feel God's love.

Alan focused on that last thought. That was the key. God did love his children, though like any parent, those children might sometimes vex him.

God had created the Spanish Flu. It was as natural as life, just as a squirrel or a bear or a man were natural and creations of God. However, just as God created the flu, he also gave man the means to defeat it. Just like Father Wunder had told him a week ago, man would be able to control the flu when God felt that they had learned the lesson they needed to learn. Alan wanted to be there and be ready to find that solution when that time arrived.

He was going to find a way to stop this flu that had killed his daughter and so many others. He was going to find a way to make sure nothing like this happened again.

Kolas walked up Baltimore Street with a bounce in his step. While the rest of the world feared the flu and feared dying, he felt happy, proud even! He was doing God's work and spreading his wrath throughout this area. People were recognizing the evil within them and returning to the way of God.

He was an avenging angel made mortal!

Kolas stopped as he prepared to enter the Central YMCA. The notice on the door announced that the public area downstairs was closed for gatherings until further noticed. He frowned. He had hoped to move some of his gatherings into the public room to avoid the cold.

If he could gather in his followers and those curious into close quarters, it would allow the flu to spread easier. The Board of Health realized things like this as well and was trying to do what they could to stop the spread of the flu.

Their efforts wouldn't work, though. God would not be stopped. The flu had only been spreading faster since the Board of Health had passed their orders.

Kolas walked through the door and smiled as he noticed the desk clerk was missing. The young man was battling his inner demons through the test of the flu. Maybe he would live. Maybe he would die. That was in God's hands. Kolas's work was to simply spread the message.

He smiled and walked up the stairs to his room.

Alan walked up the road leading into Rose Hill Cemetery. He had walked from the church rather than drive because the walk gave him time to think and remember his little girl whom he had lost forever.

The day was cold and overcast, which matched Alan's mood this afternoon.

He saw Louis Stein and Father Wunder standing near the open grave. Emily was with them, but she was sitting on a folding wooden chair. She wore a black dress that she had to buy for this occasion because her pregnancy made it impossible for her to fit into her normal clothes.

Alan had considered forbidding her to attend the funeral today, but she had gotten a lot of rest in the hospital and seemed to regain much of her strength. Exhaustion didn't seem as big a factor now when weighed against Emily being able to attend the funeral of her daughter.

Alan walked up behind her and laid his hands on Emily's shoulders and then leaned over to kiss her on the cheek.

"How do you feel?" Alan asked.

"Don't worry, I'm not exhausting myself," she said in a flat tone.

Alan shook Stein's and Father Wunder's hands. Then he looked at the closed casket sitting on the boards above the open grave. Before the sun had set, his daughter would be buried far beneath the ground.

He looked around the graveyard. Many open or freshly dug graves were within sight. Two gravediggers shoveled dirt out of the ground for another grave. It was hard to imagine people were dying fast enough to fill all of these graves. This was what the Spanish Flu had brought to the world.

Alan shook his head and turned back to stand beside Emily. They began greeting the mourners as they arrived for the open-air funeral. Alan noticed that some people were careful to maintain a safe distance from other people, so much so, that they wouldn't shake hands. It made the gathering look larger than it actually was.

As Father Wunder began to speak, Emily started sobbing. Alan put his arm around her shoulders and tried to keep from crying himself.

He focused on the casket and tried to will his daughter to rise, though he knew it was a false hope. She was gone; taken from him by the flu.

Someone coughed and the effect was as if a gun had been fired.

Father Wunder stopped speaking. Everyone in attendance turned to see who had coughed while at the same time moving away from him.

Harriet Dinning stood alone in a circle of people. Her face was red with embarrassment.

"It's all right," she said. "I'm not sick. I was just crying and it made my throat catch."

Father Wunder smiled and continued his service. Alan noticed that while the people in the crowd relaxed, the invisible boundary around Helen barely changed.

Death came with a cough nowadays and the all of the open graves and this service reminded people of that. They weren't taking any chances with their own health.

TUESDAY, OCTOBER 8, 1918

Charles Henderson shifted nervously on his chair behind the counter of the Windsor Hotel on Baltimore Street. Dawn would be coming soon, but it was always in the quiet hours before dawn that Charles felt loneliest in his work as a desk clerk for the hotel.

He stood up and walked around the lobby to stretch his legs, pausing to look out the front window onto Baltimore Street. All was quiet and dark.

He started up the stairs to the second floor. On occasion during his shift, he walked all of the halls to make sure no one was disturbing the residents and to break the monotony of the quiet hours of his shift.

The second floor was silent, as he would expect at five o'clock in the morning. He walked the length of the hall from one end to the other and then climbed the stairs to the third floor. Midway up the stairs, he heard a shot.

He froze and listened. That was it. A single shot, but it had definitely come from inside the hotel. Second or third floor?

He decided it was the third floor and ran to the landing. An elderly gentleman was standing in the hall when Charles reached the top of the stairs.

"I heard a shot," the man said.

"I heard it, too. Do you know which room?" Charles asked.

"It sounded like it was next door to me."

Charles went to the door of number 306 and listened at the door. He heard nothing from inside. He was about to knock on the door when he heard a man moan from inside.

Charles tried the door. It was locked. He pulled his key ring out of his pocket, found the master key and opened the door.

He wished he hadn't.

A man lay on the floor with a bullet hole in his stomach. A revolver

lay near his right hand. The floor and a section of the wall were covered with blood.

Charles ran forward. He grabbed a white shirt draped over a chair.
He wadded it up and pressed it against the man's wound.

"Go downstairs and call the police!" he called to the elderly man in
the hall.

"I'm not dressed for that."

Charles rolled his eyes. Now was no time for modesty. This man
could be dying. He was certainly bleeding enough to be dying.

"Then come here and hold this shirt on the man's wound and I'll
go," Charles said.

The old man obeyed and Charles rushed downstairs to call for help.

Cow watched the ambulance attendants carry the man out of the
room on a stretcher. The man was alive, but Cow wasn't sure how long
that would last. Maybe the man hadn't been serious in his suicide attempt or maybe he hadn't realized that shooting himself in the stomach
wouldn't kill him right away. It would cause him a lot of pain before
he died.

Cow walked around the room slowly and stared at the blood splat-
ters on the floor.

"How long has he been staying here?" Cow asked the desk clerk.

Charles Henderson stood off to the side of the path the police and
ambulance attendants were using as they moved through the room.

"He just took the room tonight," Charles said.

"Were you on duty?"

The clerk nodded.

"What time was that?"

"Sometime after midnight. I have it written in the guest book
downstairs."

"And what is his name?"

"Joseph Lehman."

"Do you know him?"

Charles shook his head. "He didn't say much."

"How did he act when he came in?"

The desk clerk shrugged. "Like I said, he was quiet. He seemed sad
and odd."

Cow scribbled notes into his pad. "Odd? What do you mean?"

"I tried to hand him the pen to sign the register, but he wouldn't take it from me. He made me set it on the counter and then he picked it up."

Cow noticed a pair of pants draped over a chair. He lifted the pants and found a wallet in one of the pockets. Flipping through the wallet, he pulled out a set of folded papers. He opened them and read what was written.

Lehman was the man's name. The papers Cow held were Lehman's immigration papers. Lehman had come to America from Austria a week ago. He had landed in New York Harbor.

So how had he wound up here in Cumberland?

And Austrian? Weren't the Austrians sympathizers with the Germans? Could this man be a spy?

Cow put the wallet and papers in his jacket. They would add to the investigation. Hopefully, Joseph Lehman would survive and be able to answer some other questions.

"You'll need to lock up this room until further notice from the Cumberland Police," Cow told the clerk.

"Can we clean up the wall and rugs?"

Cow shook his head. "Not yet. I'll let you know when we have what we need."

The clerk nodded.

Cow left and walked the half a dozen blocks to the Western Maryland Hospital. Helen frowned when she saw him come into the front door.

"You brought us more trouble, I see," the nurse said.

Cow held up his hands in surrender. "It's not my fault. I didn't shoot him," Cow said.

"No, I suppose not," the nurse admitted.

"You should be happy it's not another flu case."

"That's not the problem."

"Then what is the problem?"

"Your shooting victim won't let the doctors treat him. The ambulance attendants brought him in here and he was waving his hands around telling everyone not to touch him. He does not want treatment," Helen said, unable to hide the exasperation in her voice.

Lehman must have regained consciousness on the way to the hospital. The last time Cow had seen him Joseph Lehman had been unconscious.

"Did anyone tell Mr. Lehman that he'll die without medical help?"

The nurse scowled at Cow. "Of course we did, but he did attempt to kill himself. I guess he wants to finish the job."

Cow walked back to the operating room. He saw the wounded man lying on the table. Dr. Leasure was trying to talk him into an operation. The wound had been packed with bandages to stop the bleeding, but it would need to be stitched up.

The doctor saw Cow and walked over to him.

"What's wrong with him? He won't let us operate," the doctor said.

"It's a self-inflicted gunshot."

"Suicide?"

"Given his refusal for treatment, I would say so," Cow said.

Dr. Leasure nodded slowly. "He's going to die without treatment. I kept trying to tell him he'll bleed to death if we can't close him up."

"You can't do anything for him?"

The doctor shook his head. "We can do a lot for him, but not with him refusing treatment. It's his right to do so. He's got to be in a lot of pain, though."

"Has he said anything?"

"Only 'I wouldn't take the test and now God has punished me.'"

Cow rubbed his chin. "The test. I've heard that term somewhere before."

Lehman tried to sit up on the operating table and a nurse struggled to push him down. Dr. Leasure rushed over to help her.

"I've got to go, Doctor," Cow said quickly.

Cow walked back down the hallway. He now had something to occupy his mind other than the Spanish Flu. Who was Joseph Lehman and why had he shot himself? Cow had a few clues to begin his investigation with: a name, immigration papers, and the comment about the test.

Cow was sure he had had heard about a test recently and he was just as sure that it was the key to help him unravel what had driven Joseph Lehman to nearly kill himself.

Kolas walked into the Washington Street Emergency Hospital dressed in his finest suit. He stood in the front room alone until a passing nurse saw him and stopped.

"Can I help you, sir?" she asked.

Kolas smiled. "I am looking for Lorene Sears."

The woman smiled. "I was just about to leave. I'll take you to her. She's changing bed linens."

Kolas followed the woman around the corner and down a short hall. Lorene was in what had formerly been a dining room. Now there was a supply cabinet and six cots spread out through the room. Two of the cots had patients in them.

"Lorene, this gentleman was looking for you," the nurse said.

Lorene looked up from her work.

"Thank you, Janet."

The nurse left and Lorene walked over to Kolas.

"Mr. Kolas, what are you doing here?" Lorene asked.

"I wanted to see how your work is progressing."

Lorene waved her hand around the room.

"The patients are brought in and we try to make them comfortable. With those I can, I try to make sure to breathe on them as much as possible to give the flu a chance to work."

Kolas rubbed the back of his neck. "Still, the patients here all already have the flu. You are preaching to the choir."

"Oh, yes. That is specifically what this hospital is for. We opened yesterday and we already have twenty patients and more expected to arrive today. Mrs. Lichtenstein, the superintendent, is out trying to recruit more help for us," Lorene explained.

Kolas smiled. It was good to see the work of God flourishing. Yet so much more needed to be done.

"How many have died?" Kolas asked.

"Three people died overnight. We have their bodies in the basement until one of the undertakers can come and get them. The ambulances are too busy trying to transport the living to worry about the dead."

Kolas nodded and smiled. "That may be some time. I walked by Rose Hill Cemetery earlier this morning. From what I was told, they have a backlog of work. Their own gravediggers are falling sick and there are more bodies than usual to bury. Too many people have failed the test."

"You sound disappointed."

Kolas shook his head. "No, I am not. It was to be expected. The world is full of evil. That is why we have been called as angels of retribution."

Lorene frowned to hear herself called that.

Alan looked at the blood sample through the eyepieces of his microscope. He pulled back and wrote down a few notes about what he was seeing and then went back to studying the sample.

This was the third blood sample from a patient who had recovered from the flu. He didn't intend on drawing any conclusions until he studied a half a dozen samples. Then he would make some initial observations and compare them to the samples he would draw from people who had died from the flu.

Hopefully, he would find the keys he needed to create a new vaccine that would end this fear everyone was living with. Children shouldn't be afraid to play. Adults shouldn't be afraid to cough.

When he finished, Alan stepped back and stretched. He poured himself a cup of coffee and sat down at his desk to rest for a minute.

He picked up the newspaper and scanned it as he gulped down his coffee. He was surprised to see the date. He had worked through the night trying to come up with significant differences between the infected and healthy that could be distilled into a vaccine.

A short item caught his attention that the doctors were so busy that they weren't able to complete all of the death reports to the Board of Health. Alan could understand that. He realized there were probably four or five reports that he needed to fill out that were sitting on his desk.

In Alan's case, he considered his lack of promptness justified. He was looking forward not backward. He was trying to find a way to keep more people from dying not telling people that someone else had died.

He drained the cup of coffee and rubbed his eyes. He wasn't sure how much longer he could go without sleep. He should go home now and sleep and then return fresh.

He should, but how many more Annes would die while he slept?

He set the mug down and started walking back to the laboratory.

Wednesday, October 9, 1918

Kolas looked around to make sure that he was alone in the market. A quick glance up and down the aisle confirmed he was the only person in sight. He picked up an apple from the pile and spit on it. He rubbed the phlegm around with his thumb until all that anyone could notice was that this apple was shinier than those around it.

It would catch the eye of a shopper. Once it did and that shopper picked the apple up, even if she didn't buy it, the flu would spread. Germs had become a tool for God's wrath. His master would be pleased.

Kolas moved onto the oranges to do the same thing with some of them.

He had been doing this for days throughout the markets in Cumberland. Judging by how completely the flu had spread to every street and neighborhood in the city, his efforts were successful. People were learning that evil came with a price.

This town would be cleansed or it would perish.

Alan walked home from the hospital to shower and eat. The walk in the cool air helped clear his head so that he could refocus on the problem at hand. He'd spent another marathon session at the hospital looking at blood and mucus samples through a microscope, hoping to find something, anything, that would give him a clue as to what was happening.

He needed to understand his enemy.

Alan wondered whether he was doing any good. When he walked down the hallway of the hospital, he saw a first floor filled with flu patients. It was only a fraction of the cases in the city, but it was a powerful reminder to see those people. He wondered whether they would live or die. To often the answer was death. Helen had told him that Allegany Hospital and the Washington Street Emergency Hospital were similarly taxed.

They might have been able to handle the caseload if a lot of the nurses and doctors hadn't come down with the flu themselves. Between Allegany and Western Maryland Hospital, a third of the nurses and doctors had caught the flu, despite using gloves and gauze masks around the patients. Worse yet, four of them had died.

Louis Stein had told Alan that the undertakers and gravediggers were falling behind in their work. They were shorthanded because so many of them had the flu and they were having to deal with a higher number of deaths than they typically saw. The local cemeteries were beginning to look like freshly plowed fields.

No one fully understood how the Spanish Flu was transmitted so how could it be stopped? Why did one person in a house catch the flu while another person didn't? Why was Pfeiffer's Bacillus present now in the deadly form of the flu while it had been missing in the strain from this spring?

Alan needed answers to those questions. If he could answer any one of them, he might be able to stop this flu from spreading.

He was surprised by silence when he entered the house. Emily liked to play records while she was working. She hadn't fully overcome the grief of Anne's death.

"Emily!" Alan called wearily.

"I'm in the bedroom," she responded.

Alan walked up the stairs and into the bedroom. He stopped when he saw Emily lying on the bed. It didn't even look as if she had gotten up at all this morning.

"Is something wrong?" Alan asked.

"I'm just tired from the pregnancy. I woke up this morning and ached all over so I decided I would rest," Emily told him.

Ache? Alan worked hard to suppress a shudder.

He walked over and sat next to his wife on the bed. He noticed a thin sheen of sweat on her forehead as he laid his hand on her forehead. She was running a fever.

He took a deep breath.

"You've got the flu, Emily," he said.

"What? Oh, no, Alan. No." She started to cry.

He stood up. "I'm going to get you some aspirin powder to help with the achy muscles. I also want to make sure you drink as much fluid as possible."

He had been using a variety of drugs at the hospital to treat the flu symptoms and give the patients some relief. Aspirin and morphine for pain. Codeine for coughing. In the extreme cases, he used digitalis and atropine to stimulate a weak body in the hopes of keeping a dying patient alive.

Alan walked around the room and opened the two windows partially to get fresh air coming into the room. It made the room colder, but his wife needed the fresh air.

"Alan, don't leave," Emily said.

He grabbed her hand and patted it. "I won't. I'm here to treat you."

The problem was he had treated his daughter, too. He had failed Anne. Would he fail Emily as well? He certainly wasn't sure what he could do to treat the illness. All he could do was combat Emily's symptoms and help her body overcome the flu.

Cow walked out of the Fort Cumberland Hotel's kitchen and stepped onto the street. He blinked in the sunlight and wrote a couple notes in his pad. Then he shoved the pad into his jacket pocket.

The street was nearly deserted. It looked almost like a ghost town. Too many people were sick with the flu and the rest were trying to hide away in their homes. As if walls could stop the flu. Still, it made walking a beat easier. Not much crime would happen when even criminals were afraid to go out on the street.

It also gave him more time to investigate Joseph Lehman's history. The immigrant had been working as a cook at the Fort Cumberland Hotel for a few days until he had been fired because of his unusual behavior. The workers in the hotel had told Cow that Lehman had been paranoid about catching the flu. Had that driven him to act oddly? Had Lehman caught the flu and shot himself in his delirium? It had happened to a man in Hancock, a town on the western edge of Washington County to the east of Allegany County. Cow had read the notice in the newspaper today.

He headed toward Western Maryland Hospital. He had called earlier to check on Lehman's condition and been told that the man had finally consented to be treated late last night. He was weak, but he would survive. Now, maybe, Cow could get some answers from him about what happened.

On the corner next to the Central YMCA, Cow saw Kolas standing on a box preaching loudly to a crowd that was beginning to gather around him. The crowd grew and began to spill into the street. Cow couldn't do much about Kolas's preaching, but if the crowd was large enough that it began to block traffic, he would be able to disperse them.

As Cow walked past the crowd, he heard Kolas shout, "Even now the results of the test are coming in. God has pronounced judgment on the world and found so many of those in it wanting. He has struck his blow against the evil in the world. Are you still arrogant enough to believe you can face his judgment alone? No, brothers and sisters, only those with his mark have a chance to survive."

Cow stopped walking.

Test?

Could this be the test that Lehman feared? He was paranoid about catching the flu. If he had been listening to Kolas, he would have been convinced that God was killing evil people with the flu. If Lehman considered himself evil, he would have believed it was only a matter of time before he died.

Cow shook his head.

If Kolas was inciting these types of actions among the people who listened to him, then Cow would have a reason to revoke his street license. Nothing would please him more. Dealing with the Spanish Flu was bad enough, but if Kolas was adding to the fear in order to can power over people, Cow could deal with that.

He had shut down some of the roughest saloons in this city. He would take on this man and control the fear if that was what was needed to end this madness.

Thursday,
October 10, 1918

Alan walked from his home to the market where his wife typically shopped for groceries. Emily was still sick, but he had chosen to care for her at home.

Although the first floor of the Western Maryland Hospital had been set aside for flu patients, it was already full. As soon as one bed became available – and it was all to often because the person occupying it had died – a new flu patient filled it within minutes.

Besides, Alan wasn't sure that he wanted her in a room full of people with the flu. It might hamper her recovery. He wanted to care for Emily where she would be the most comfortable and that would be in her own home in her own bedroom.

As Alan walked along Columbia Street, he was surprised to see three girls skipping rope. Most people stayed off the streets lately, particularly those who were doing normal things like these girls. He paused in his walk to watch them and enjoy the sense of normalcy.

They reminded him of Anne and Alan wanted to remember his daughter.

One of the girls held each end of a long rope and spun it around while the third girl stood in the middle and jumped the rope and sang a little chant. Alan froze when he realized what the girls were singing.

"I had a little bird.

"Its name was Enza.

"I opened the window.

"And in flew Enza."

Influenza.

Spanish Flu had already become a part of children's rhymes just as the Black Plague had been immortalized in "Ring Around the Rosey."

Alan shook his head and continued walking. So much for things being normal.

At the market, Alan looked at the shopping list he had written out. He picked up a basket and started looking for vegetables, soup and the other items. He would have to stop by the bakery for a loaf of bread a little later. He moved back and forth between the four aisles as he found the items on the list of groceries. It wasn't the most-efficient way to shop, but he wasn't familiar with the store.

As Alan moved around an end cap to look for produce, he saw Kolas standing in the aisle. Alan stopped and drew back so he was almost entirely behind the end cap. He watched the man in black looking at the apples.

This was the man who was raising hysteria about the flu, as if it needed any help to scare people. Kolas didn't look threatening or unusual. He didn't look angry or crazed. He was dressed in a black suit and looked like the preacher he called himself.

Alan watched as Kolas spit on the apple, rubbed the saliva around and then sat the apple back on the pile. Alan's eyes widened and he had to force himself not to charge out into the aisle and confront Kolas. He wouldn't be able to do anything to stop him.

But he could stop what Kolas wanted to happen.

Alan hurried to the front of the store and asked the clerk for a paper bag. Then he slid the contaminated apple into the bag, careful not to touch it himself.

Was this one of the ways that the flu was spreading so easily throughout the city? Had Kolas been helping it spread on purpose?

Alan quickly paid for his groceries and the apple and then hurried back to the house. He left the groceries sitting on the table in the kitchen and took the apple to the hospital. If he was right, Kolas could be arrested for attempted murder or something along that line.

When he came into the entrance, Helen called to him, "Dr. Hyatt wants to see you."

"That's good because I want to see him, too."

"He's in room nine."

Alan hurried down the corridor to room nine. He was surprised to see that Hyatt wasn't attending a patient in the room. He was the patient.

The doctor lay in the bed with his eyes closed and looking pale. His perspiration plastered his hair down on his head.

"Dr. Hyatt, what happened?" Alan asked.

Hyatt opened his eyes. He smiled slightly. "I caught the flu. What does it look like happened?"

Alan held up the brown paper bag. "I think I may know how some of the flu is being transmitted...at least one of the ways it is being transmitted."

"What's in there?" Dr. Hyatt lifted a shaky hand and pointed to the brown paper bag.

"An apple," Alan said.

"It will take more than an apple to keep the doctor away from me."

Alan shook his head. "No, I saw Kolas — you know, the street preacher who's been saying that the flu needs to spread. He spit on this apple."

"Spit?"

Alan nodded. "If he has the flu germs in his saliva, guess what happens to the person who unknowingly picks up this apple?"

Despite his sickness, Hyatt managed to sit upright in the bed. "Damn him! Can you prove what you're saying?"

"I'm going to the lab to see if I can detect Pfeiffer's Bacillus on the apple. If it's there, then I can get the police involved. They can arrest Kolas and get him off the streets."

Hyatt relaxed and lay back down. "Good, good for you. Get him. Anyone who tries to spread this flu is crazy and should be locked up."

"I'm going to take this to the lab then."

Hyatt reached out to Alan. "Wait a moment, please, Alan." When Alan turned back, Hyatt said, "I wanted to apologize for delaying so long to do anything about this. I just didn't think it would take hold here. I really didn't."

Alan nodded slowly. "You weren't the only one."

"And now that it has and we're alert to it, we don't have the staff to deal with it. You can't win with this flu. It attacks from both sides and the newspapers say you can't win a two-front war."

Alan knew what Hyatt was talking about. The hospital was full of patients but it looked nearly deserted of doctors and nurses. The flu increases the number of patients while at the same time decreasing the number of medical personnel to deal with the problem.

"We'll do what we can and that will have to be enough," Alan said.

Hyatt nodded and closed his eyes.

Alan rushed down to the lab. He put on gloves and peeled a patch of skin from the apple. He prepared a section and placed it under the microscope. The first three slides yielded nothing, but the fourth slide showed plenty of Pfeiffer's Bacillus.

Alan sighed.

He picked up the telephone and placed a call to the police department.

Cow was angry enough to hit something or someone. Chief Eyerman had told the police officers to be on the lookout for Kolas and arrest him. The man was intentionally contaminating people with the flu! Two police officers had died now from the flu not to mention the hundreds of others who had died throughout the county. How many of them would still be alive if Kolas hadn't been around?

Cow also blamed himself earlier for not realizing the danger Kolas was to the city. He should have been able to piece things together from what Lorene and Joseph Lehman had said.

Kolas was "testing" people by contaminating them. If they survived the flu, it was the will of God. If they died, it was because they were evil.

Cow should have realized this earlier. How many times had he seen Kolas over the past couple weeks? And all the time the man had been spreading the flu right under Cow's nose. Maybe Cow was as stupid as people believed him to be.

He was going to find Kolas, though, and when he did he would put a stop to one way the flu was spreading through Cumberland.

FRIDAY,
OCTOBER 11, 1918

Cow searched for Kolas as he walked his beat faster and longer. He took different routes and altered his pace in case the man had begun timing his preaching around how often Cow passed a certain area on his beat. Cow talked to people he met and asked them if they had seen the street preacher. He told shopkeepers to call the station if they saw Kolas.

Cow didn't find Kolas anywhere. It was as if the man knew he was being sought by police and was avoiding them.

What Cow did hear about was the rumors about the flu's origins.

A city commissioner stopped him outside of Rosenbaum's and said, "Have you had any luck finding that street preacher?"

"No, sir. Have you seen him?" Cow replied respectfully. He was always respectful to a man who could have him fired.

The commissioner shook his head. "No, but I think he's not the problem. You should be searching out German spies like that man in the Windsor Hotel who shot himself the other day."

"He was Austrian."

"What?"

"The man who shot himself was Austrian, not German," Cow corrected him.

The commissioner shrugged. "Austrian. German. They are both enemies of our country. I heard that this isn't the flu we're dealing with at all. It's that damned German germ warfare like mustard gas."

Cow doubted that, but he had also wondered if Joseph Lehman was a spy. "How would they get such a thing over here?"

"I heard that one of those German submarines crept across the ocean into Boston Harbor and released the germs into the air during the night. I personally don't believe that because I don't think the Germans are smart enough to get by the good old U.S. Navy."

"Then why do you think it's Germans who caused the epidemic?"

"It's that Bayer Aspirin they've been sending us. They've mixed something with the aspirin powder to make us sick. That's how the flu's been able to spread so far and so fast," the commissioner said sincerely.

Cow tried to keep from rolling his eyes. And people thought that he was dumb!

"I'll keep that in mind, sir, but Dr. Keener said he saw Kolas spreading the flu on apples in markets around town. He even tested the apples to be sure."

"How did he do that?"

"He spit on them."

The commissioner's eyes widened. "Now who would spit on apples? That's disgusting." The commissioner arched his eyebrows. "Now Keener. He's German, don't you know. He changed his name when he graduated medical school. Dr. Hyatt told me. You can't trust what he's saying. He's trying to protect his homeland by trying to divert our attention from the real problem."

"I'll keep that in mind," Cow said carefully. "For now, I have to keep searching for Kolas."

"No, not Kolas. Keener and his German friends. Those are the ones you need to watch out for."

"My orders from the chief are to find Kolas."

"Well then, you what the chief told you, Officer Lewis. It's good to follow orders, but I'll have to have a talk with Chief Eyerman about the real problem we're facing."

Cow walked off and crossed Baltimore Street as soon as he far enough away for it to be polite. He didn't want to take a chance that the commissioner might have more ideas to tell him.

The other problem that Cow was running into was that some of the saloons were opening up again as quietly as they could. They put heavy drapes in their front windows and added coffee and juices to their menus so they could argue that they weren't operating saloons. Of course, very little of the drinks served were actually coffee or juice. It also didn't matter what they served. The fact that they were operating put people close to each other … too close.

Cow realized that he could continue to shut them down, but people were going to find other ways to get drunk or gather. It didn't help that there was a popular rumor going around that since alcohol was used to kill germs in hospitals that alcohol in a person's insides would kill the flu germs. Cow had to admit that it sounded a lot more feasible than the commissioner's idea of German espionage.

During times of stress, people were willing to grab onto any possible solution. Cow just hoped that the "solutions" wouldn't make matters worse.

Alan looked at the paper that the nurse had just handed him. It was a long list of supplies for another emergency hospital that was going to open.

"Where is this hospital going to be?" Alan asked.

"The person I spoke to at the Red Cross said this one would be on the main floor at the B&O YMCA and may expand to the other floors if needed," Helen said.

That meant it would be on Virginia Avenue. That was good. South Cumberland could use a little extra help in dealing with the flu.

"Then it will only remain on the main floor for about an hour before it needs to expand. We couldn't meet the demand for beds with fifty Western Maryland Hospitals."

"No, sir," Helen said.

Alan turned his head and stared at her. "When's the last time you slept?"

Helen hesitated. "Yesterday."

Alan shook his head. "Use the cot in my office and sleep."

"I'll be fine."

"You look about ready to fall asleep standing up. You won't be any help to me if you get so weak you catch the flu."

"Yes, sir."

"Are we still down ten nurses?"

Helen shook her head. "It's fourteen now and three of our nurses have died."

Alan closed his eyes and sighed. "I'd send flowers but their families would probably be afraid to open their doors for the delivery."

"Yes, sir."

"Did the Red Cross know that the state hospital train arrived today? It will be down by the YMCA," Alan asked.

The B&O Special was a four-car train that the State of Maryland had equipped as a mobile hospital. There were hospital beds, an ambulance, a fully-equipped laboratory and additional staff. More important to Alan was that the hospital came with a fully-stocked pharmacy. The local pharmacies were running low on the drugs needed to treat the typical flu.

The nurse shrugged. "I don't know. He didn't say anything about it. He did say he was also helping equip an emergency hospital in Laughlin's Hall in Piedmont."

"Okay. I'll put these items in a truck and drive them over to the YMCA. I can help the staff there get ready for their patients. I want to make sure they keep the rooms as ventilated as possible."

He also wanted to see what information about the flu might be gleaned from the doctors with the state health train. He would stop in there after he was finished at the YMCA.

"You," Alan pointed at Helen. "Go get some sleep. Doctor's orders."

The nurse walked away and Alan went back to his work, checking on the flu patients. He'd found that with Dr. Hyatt and many of the other doctors ill, the responsibility of running the hospital had fallen on him by default. It wasn't that he had any seniority at the hospital. He was simply here more than anyone else so the nurses – what few are left – brought their problems to him.

When Alan was ready to take a break, he piled a gurney high with supplies on the Red Cross list and loaded them onto the hospital's truck. Then he grabbed the keys and drove off.

His first stop was at the house to check on Emily. She was still weak, but she seemed stable. He washed her face with a wet cloth and fed her some soup. Then he set a glass and a large pitcher of water next to her bed.

"I want to see all of this gone when I stop by again," Alan told his wife.

"That's a lot of water," Emily said weakly.

"Yes, it is but you need to keep from dehydrating. I'm going to have you drinking water constantly if I can."

"I'll be spending more time in the bathroom than in the bed," she complained.

"Fine."

"Says you. You don't feel like an elephant when you walk."

"Says Dr. Keener. If we can keep the water moving through your body, it will keep your system flushed and hopefully wash out any toxins that might hinder your recovery."

"Yes, doctor," Emily said mildly.

He kissed her on the forehead. As he started to walk away, Emily asked, "When will all this fear end, Alan?"

He stopped and turned back to her. He wanted to lie to her and give her a reassuring answer, but it was too easy to do.

"I don't know. If the Spanish Flu acts like regular flu, I would say, at worst, it will end when the flu season ends."

"But," Emily said, sensing additional conditions.

"But it doesn't act like typical influenza all the time."

"Will we all die?"

"No, we all won't die and you won't die," he said firmly.

"How do you know?"

Alan tapped his head. "Logic."

"What logic?"

"Every living organism wants to live. The flu virus is a living organism and it needs us to live, therefore, it won't kill all of us."

Emily said, "Your logic has a problem."

"What's that?"

"If it needs us, why kill us at all?"

"Because we're individuals. What's safe for one person may not be safe for someone else. And you are strong so you will survive." Alan hugged his wife tightly for a few moments and then left.

He drove the truck over to South Cumberland, scolding himself for not staying longer when Emily needed him. She wanted him at home with her, but he could do more good for her out here, searching for those elusive answers.

The B&O YMCA was a four-floor wooden-sided building. Depending on how many people were living there, it had plenty of room to serve as an emergency hospital. And he doubted many of the residents would stay once they found out it had become a hospital for people with Spanish Flu.

Alan unloaded the boxes from the truck and carried them into the main floor of the YMCA. Two nurses who were in charge of preparing the hospital began unpacking the supplies. They had already been setting up additional cots in the empty rooms and common areas. Alan wondered how long these two nurses would work before they got scared of all the death or caught the flu themselves.

Alan was nearly finished unloading the truck when he saw Kolas. The man was speaking to a group of people from the corner of Virginia Avenue and Second Avenue. Alan couldn't hear what Kolas was saying, but he was sure the man was trying to convince people to allow themselves to be infected by the flu.

Alan hurried back into the hospital and called the police from the YMCA's telephone.

"This is Dr. Keener. The man you're searching for, Kolas, is in South Cumberland. I saw him speaking on the corner of Virginia Avenue and Second Avenue," Alan told the desk sergeant.

"We'll get someone out that as soon as we can, doctor, but we're a little shorthanded here, too," the desk sergeant told him.

"If this man isn't captured, I would guess that you'll be even more shorthanded before this flu epidemic is over," Alan replied.

He hung up the phone and went back outside. He walked down the street and stood on the outskirts of the crowd around Kolas. If the police didn't get here in time, Alan would follow the street preacher until he could alert the police again. They couldn't risk losing track of him and allowing him to contaminate even more people.

Arresting Kolas might not stop the flu in the city, but it would slow its spread down and judging by some of Kolas's rhetoric, it should also decrease some of the panic about the flu.

Alan stood on the edge of crowd listening to Kolas try to encourage people to test their commitment to God. He wasn't saying outright that the test would be catching the flu and surviving it. He probably knew how quickly he would lose his crowd if they knew he wanted them to risk death.

A police car parked along the curb further up Virginia Avenue and an officer stepped onto the sidewalk. He began walking toward Kolas, casually swinging his baton as if nothing was wrong.

Kolas saw the officer and quickly wound up his speech. He moved away in the opposite direction, putting the crowd between the policeman and himself.

Kolas knew the police were hunting him and he was going to get away!

Alan hurried to where Kolas was coming out of the crowd and grabbed the man.

"What are you doing?" Kolas asked.

"The police want to talk to you," Alan told him.

"I don't want to talk to them."

Kolas tried to pull free, but Alan held him tight. He couldn't let the street preacher get away. The man was too dangerous.

"You're going to wait for the police," Alan said.

"I will not."

"You don't have a choice."

Kolas thought for a moment. "I think you are wrong there. God always provides a way for his servants to do his work."

Kolas suddenly spat in Alan's face. The wad of phlegm hit Alan on the cheek. Alan was so startled that he let go of Kolas and jumped back. All he could think of was that Kolas's saliva had had Pfeiffer's Bacillus! Kolas was trying to infect him with the Spanish Flu.

Alan grabbed at his handkerchief from his pocket and wiped his face clean. He'd have to swab his face with alcohol to disinfect himself. When he looked up, Kolas was gone.

He threw the handkerchief to the ground in anger.

Saturday, October 12, 1918

The crowd at city hall surprised Alan. He hadn't seen this many healthy people together indoors in weeks. They had chosen to gather in the evening, almost as if they wanted to hide their meeting under the cover of darkness. He followed the flow of people up the stairs into the main floor of the city hall and then to the council room on the second floor.

Alan was pleased to see that everyone seemed a bit nervous about having a meeting indoors. Some of them actually held handkerchiefs over their mouths when they talked to one another. It meant that they were being cautious about passing the flu along and they should be since they were primarily doctors. Dr. Thomas Koon had called to meeting of the medical profession in the city to discuss a way to deal with the problems caused by the flu. He had been appointed as an act-ing assistant surgeon of the United States Public Health Service and he was taking his position seriously.

The council room was full and Alan noticed that all of the doors and windows were kept open. He saw doctors, Red Cross officers, Sergeant General Blue of the Public Health Service and officers of the various organizations in town represented in the group.

Thomas looked at the clock on the wall, said something to the doc-tor next to him and then stood up. The crowd quieted down.

"Okay, ladies and gentlemen, let's get this meeting going. I'd like to keep it as short as possible. It wouldn't do much good to come up with a plan to fight the Spanish Flu and then have it fall apart because everyone we need to make it work got sick," Thomas said.

The comment got some light laughter, but most people were too nervous about Koon being right to appreciate the humor.

"You all know what we're facing so I won't recap it. I met this morning with Mr. D. Z. Dunott who is the chief surgeon for the Potomac District of the United States Railroad Administration…" Thomas nodded toward Dunott and he stood up. "…and Mr. E. V. Millholland who is the chief medical examiner for the Baltimore and Ohio Railroad and in charge of the Maryland State Hospital Train, which arrived yesterday evening to help us." Koon nodded toward Millholland who held up his hand and waved to the crowd.

"We met and talked about a plan that most of you have probably heard me talking about since this epidemic hit our city. We are short-handed and have doctors running all over creation to answer medical calls, sometimes going to the same calls to treat patients. We need a systematic way of cooperation to attend the calls. I think we have developed that."

A murmur of assent rose from the crowd.

"We've divided Cumberland and surrounding areas into six wards with the doctors for the negroes covering all areas. In this way, each zone will have twenty-four-hour coverage and the doctors won't be criss-crossing each other and duplicating each other's efforts. We don't have enough healthy doctors to waste our efforts like that," said Thomas.

He pointed to a large map of Cumberland and the surrounding area that was sitting on an easel. The map had been marked off in zones and labeled one through six. Thomas then read off the names of the doctors that would be covering each zone.

When he finished, he said, "You can select your rotation as a group, but you need to submit a list of who will be covering when to each hospital so the operators know whom to call."

"Are the hospitals filled?" one of the doctors asked.

Koon shook his head. "No. We have opened another emergency hospital in the Mertens home near both of the hospitals. It will be able to handle any overflow from either hospital for the time being. The Red Cross is running it and Mabel Avers will serve as superintendent. Mabel, stand up and let everyone see you."

A middle-aged woman near the front of the room stood up and turned around so that everyone could see her.

When she sat, Thomas said, "We also have the state hospital train in the B&O rail yard. It has seven cars with a fully stocked pharmacy. More importantly, the train staff adds nine doctors and twelve nurses to our dwindling numbers."

A quick calculation told Alan it wasn't nearly enough, but it would help.

Excited talk broke out among the crowd at hearing additional help was here. Alan knew that the extra staff would be a big help in trying to keep up with all of the flu cases. It would be nice to sleep, too.

"We also need to get word out to the public that anyone needing emergency help should call a special telephone number we've arranged through the telephone company that will only service our emergency calls. That number is four-five-three. Remember it and make sure that you tell everyone you can talk to what this number is," said Thomas.

Some people wrote the phone number down.

"I told you that I would keep this meeting short and so I'll let the ward physicians get together in your smaller groups and organize yourselves. We're are dealing with a modern-day plague here and we must persevere or we will be overcome."

The crowd quickly broke up almost as if they were anxious to be away from each other to avoid being infected with the flu.

Cow sat in a chair next to the window of his apartment above McKenney's Tavern on Centre Street. He watched a man ride by in a carriage, but other than that, the street was deserted.

He lifted the bottle to his lips and took a healthy swig. The whiskey burned going down his throat but it settled nicely into his stomach and warmed him up.

People were dying and he couldn't do anything to stop them. People were afraid to live, to go out, to be near another person.

He had let Kolas roam free when Cow could have stopped the flu by arresting him. How many times had Cow seen him over the past few weeks? A dozen? More? Now no one knew where the street preacher was and everyone wanted a cure for the flu.

Cow had found the cure. Get good and drunk. If alcohol could kill germs on the outside of your skin, then copious amounts could finish the germs off that were inside your body, including the ones that brought the flu. He didn't necessarily believe the theory he had heard on the street, but it was as good a reason as any to get drunk nowadays.

Not to mention that the booze made him feel less afraid. He actually felt pretty good.

Sunday,
October 13, 1918

Cow woke up at dawn and groaned at the brightness of the sunlight coming through his bedroom window. He lay in his bed with his arm thrown over his head.

When would he learn that the pleasure of drinking the night before was not worth how he felt the next morning? Maybe he was as stupid as a cow.

Cow staggered out of bed in his nightshirt. He paused to look at himself in the mirror and couldn't remember dressing himself for bed. He stumbled across the floor and down the hall to his bathroom where he splashed water on his face. He shook an aspirin tablet out of a glass bottle. He held it up and stared at it between his fingers. So a city commissioner thought this was poisoned? Well, Cow had taken probably two dozen or more over the past year and none of them had killed him yet. He popped it in his mouth and swallowed it with a gulp of water. His mouth felt so dry that it seemed to absorb the water he swallowed before it could get down his throat.

He was more tempted to stay in bed than be up and dressed. His bed and thick quilt looked so inviting. He just wanted to fall back into it.

That wouldn't do today.

He forced himself to shower. He kept the water cool to help wake himself up. When he finished, he was shivering, but he was alert. He quickly dried off and dressed in his only suit.

His usual tavern stop on Mechanic Street was open but it only had seating outside. It was chilly since it was still too early in the morning for the sun to heat things up. Still, Cow wasn't alone when he sat down to eat at one of the six small tables. Paul's Tavern usually didn't have any outside seating, but Paul Trimble had decided to work around the health order, which the Board of Health hadn't protested.

Paul's wife, Maxine, came out to take Cow's order. She was a middle-aged woman whose small frame was beginning to take on more weight.

"The usual, Cow?" she asked.

"Can you make sure that it's hot? I'll need it to keep warm this morning," Cow said as he rubbed his hands together.

Maxine laughed.

The fried eggs, bacon, toast, home fries and black coffee came out a few minutes later. Cow held his hands over the food to warm them and then dug into the food.

He surprised himself at how hungry he was. Then he realized that he hadn't eaten last night because he had been drinking.

He finished up the meal and left a quarter on the plate to pay for his food and the tip for Maxine. Then he started walking south on Mechanic Street and up the hill toward Emmanuel Episcopal Church on Washington Street. It stood like a beacon on the hill where Fort Cumberland had once stood nearly two centuries ago. It was where Cumberland had been born and grown to be the city of almost thirty thousand people that it was now.

He felt a bit uneasy walking into the church because he hadn't attended a service for months and then only been because his mother had asked him when the last time he had gone to church. That had been back in June. He had gone the Sunday after she had asked and then not again until now.

Cow just hadn't been interested in church and God. Neither one had a place in his life. That had been when the world seemed normal. Or as normal as the world could seem when it was at war. Even then, it was still far more normal than fighting an unseen enemy and wondering if the person speaking to you would kill you because his words carried the flu with them.

The chapel was closed and folding wooden seats had been set up outside on the lawn. Cow was surprised to see more seats filled than had been when he had attended church back in the summer and indoors. People were worried about the flu, or rather, they were worried about dying from the flu. They wanted reassurance from God that they would live to see tomorrow.

Was that why Cow had come today?

He wasn't sure. He had felt a longing to be here. Maybe he was searching for answers as to why God was doing this to the world. Wasn't there enough death in the world right now with the war going on? Why did he have to unleash something like the Spanish Flu?

Cow bowed his head and prayed silently, "Heavenly Father, why? Why do you allow something like the flu that you can control to rampage when we're already killing so many people? Are we such a disappointment to you that you don't want us here anymore?"

"No. He won't stop the flu."

Cow looked up. Reverend Harvey McConnell stood next to him. The older man was wearing his vestments and had paused in his walk down the aisle to makeshift pulpit.

"What, Reverend?" Cow asked.

"I saw you praying, Cow, and I assumed you were praying for what everyone is praying for lately, especially those who haven't been to church in a while."

Cow accepted the mild rebuke without comment.

"That wasn't what I was praying for. I was wondering why he would allow something like the Spanish Flu to happen."

Reverend McConnell smiled. "That's an easy one to answer. Why does he allow floods and tornadoes to happen? Why does he allow it to rain or snow? Why has he allowed the Sabbath to be cold today when we cannot meet inside?"

"I thought that was just how the world worked."

The reverend nodded and smiled. "It is. And when nature sometimes gets a bit overwhelmed, the results are disasters like tornadoes, earthquakes and floods. God created nature as the engine to run this world and it has run the world relatively well. The Spanish Flu is something natural like mosquitoes or you or me. It was created when certain things in nature happened, just like any other disease. Nature will correct itself when the results are excessive. It simply takes a little time."

"I hope so."

"There's no hope about it. It will happen."

"But will you or I be around to see it?"

"If it is God's will for us to be here, then we will be."

Cow nodded.

Reverend McConnell patted Cow on the shoulder and continued his walk to the front of the open-air chapel to begin the service.

Cow sat on the chair and listened to service. As he did, he felt the tension he had been under lately leech out of his body. It would probably return in a few hours, but for the moment, he simply enjoyed the peace he felt.

This was where he needed to be now.

Monday,
October 14, 1918

Lorene dipped the cloth in a pan of water, wrung it out, and then wiped the brow of a middle-aged woman suffering from the Spanish Flu. The woman moaned slightly at the coolness of the water. It must have felt good against her skin, which was burning up at one-hundred-and-four degrees.

Lorene could remember little of her own experience with the flu. The memories were lost in a haze of fever and grief. Had she looked like this woman? Had she suffered in this way and enjoyed the small joy of cold water against her hot skin?

Lorene feared for this woman whose name she didn't even know. She was simply a woman who had collapsed on Washington Street near the emergency hospital. Lorene had seen her this morning as she walked across the street for her nursing shift. How long the woman had lain in the road Lorene didn't know. Lorene had dragged the woman into the hospital and put her to bed.

Prospects did not look good for the woman to survive her bout with the flu. She was struggling to live now and probably would die alone because people were afraid of anyone with the flu. No one wanted to die like this.

Did I infect this woman? Lorene wondered.

Thoughts like that haunted her as she worked now to save people's lives. Had she caused their misery? Had she brought death's attention to them?

Kolas would be happy, but Lorene felt no joy in the thought.

So many people were dying. It seemed as if every time Lorene walked across the street from the home where the emergency workers were staying, another patient had died in his or her sleep. Rarely did their deaths look as if they had been peaceful. Their faces many times were twisted in agony and their eyes stared out at nothing yet still filled with fear even in death.

What had they seen in their last moments?

Lorene felt a hand on her and jumped. Then she turned and saw Mrs. Lichtenstein.

"Are you all right, dear?" the older woman asked.

"Yes, ma'am. I just drifted off for a moment."

"I can understand that. We're all tired, but you're doing a wonderful job. You have a kind touch and that's what these people need the most."

Lorene liked the older woman. She was devoted to caring for the sick and injured. Her compassion showed through in her words and expressions.

"I don't feel like I'm doing any good. So many people are dying," Lorene said.

"You're right. We are more caregivers than healers in this situation. Everyone feels powerless in the face of the flu."

"Then we aren't doing any good."

Mrs. Lichtenstein held up a finger. "I didn't say that. How many would die if we weren't attending them? How many of those that did die did so with a friendly face nearby rather than alone and scared? This woman would have died if she had remained in the street much longer. You have helped her. Sometimes our efforts are small when considered separately, but each kindness builds on the others and together we make a difference."

Lorene shrugged. "I just don't know."

Mrs. Lichtenstein reached out and touched Lorene's head. She frowned and pressed her hand against Lorene's forehead.

"I want you to find an empty cot and lay down and sleep for a while," the hospital superintendent ordered Lorene.

"But I just came on duty."

Mrs. Lichtenstein shook her head. "You're running a fever, dear. I'm worried that you might be catching the flu yourself."

Lorene's eyes went wide. "I can't be. I just got over it."

"Who can say how this flu will act, but you're showing the symptoms. Maybe you just need some rest or maybe your first bout with the flu wasn't severe enough for your body to build up its immunities or maybe you never fully got over it."

Lorene didn't know what to say. She looked down at the woman on the cot and wondered if she would be like her in a few days. Lorene didn't want to die. Not anymore.

Now she had a reason to live. If she couldn't save Robert, she could save others who had the same thing that had killed him.

She'd grieved over Robert, but he would not want her to die. He would want her to fight back and live. Calvin had convinced her of that.

Mrs. Lichtenstein took Lorene by the arm and led her into another ward room where there was an empty cot. She pulled back the sheet.

"Lay down, Lorene. Try to sleep, but if you can't sleep right now, pray."

WEDNESDAY, OCTOBER 16, 1918

Alan had read the newspaper reports and had heard the hopeful talk among the nurses and doctors in the hospital. The number of new flu cases was dropping off. He could almost feel a release of some of the tension that everyone was feeling from wondering who would be the next to die. Alan had even seen the reduction in his own work.

Maybe the flu had worked its way through the county, but Alan was only worried about what was happening to Emily. She was the focus of his attention now that he didn't have to worry so much about new cases of the flu and covering open shifts at the hospital.

He was spending more time with her now, but he hadn't been able to help her condition. She was in the hospital now. He was just fighting the symptoms that appeared in his wife. Cool cloths and aspirin to fight her fever. Lots of fluids to fight her dehydration. Fresh air to keep the germs away.

Alan placed his stethoscope on his wife's chest and listened. He still heard fluid moving in her lungs. That worried him. He remembered what Sarah Jenkins lungs had looked like during her autopsy. She had drowned in her own fluids.

He couldn't let that happen to Emily and the baby.

What choice did he have though?

He had her continually blowing her nose and coughing up any phlegm she could. Anything she could do to dry out her tissues would retard the fluid.

He was dosing her with mild amounts of aspirin to ease her pain. He was not trying to cure the influenza but to keep it from developing into pneumonia or bronchitis and pray that she wouldn't be one of the small percentage of people who died.

He was also using Vick's Vapor Rub liberally on Emily in addition to hot towels to help ease her breathing. It was a new product that was supposed to help clear the lungs, but it made the room smell of menthol and camphor even with the windows open.

When her condition had worsened, Alan had broken down and brought her to the hospital where he could watch her. Like he had with Anne.

"How is she, Doctor?" Helen asked from the doorway.

Alan looked over his shoulder. "About the same. I guess that is good news nowadays. How are you feeling?"

Helen shrugged. "I'm still tired, but I'm not sick."

"Good. You need to take care of yourself."

"So do you. You need to go home and sleep."

Alan shook his head. "I'll be fine."

"Maybe, but walking around groggy won't help Emily. Dr. Bromwell's here. Go home and sleep. Nurse's orders."

Alan smiled and then nodded. He kissed Emily on the cheek and then stood up to walk out of the hospital room.

Helen said, "Don't forget your coat. It's getting colder."

Alan chuckled, the first time in a long time. It just seemed so absurd to worry about catching a cold when they were facing the deadliest influenza known to man.

"Thank you," he said, but he didn't mean for being reminded about wearing his coat.

It was cold outside and gray. The weather matched his mood, but he was glad he was wearing his overcoat nonetheless. He kept his collar up and his hands shoved into his pockets as he walked along Columbia Street at a quick clip.

A rotten tomato hit him in the chest spraying juice in his face.

"Go home, Hessian!"

Alan looked up. Lucille Connelly stood on the porch of her house. A bucket of vegetables sat on the porch railing in front of her. She pulled another tomato from the bucket and threw it at Alan. He dodged this one and it landed on the street behind him.

"What are you doing, Mrs. Connelly?"

"It's you! You brought the plague here!" she shouted.

"I didn't. I've been trying everything I know to stop it."

"Liar! It wasn't enough that you took my husband, but you had to take my son, too."

Phillip Connelly had died in France two months ago. Eight-year-old Jacob Connelly had died from the Spanish Flu two days ago.

"I'm very sorry about your loss, but I had nothing to do with either one of their deaths."

"Liar! You're a German. Did you think we wouldn't find out? Germans killed Phillip with their guns and they killed Jacob with their germ warfare."

"It's not germ warfare. It's the flu."

"Liar! That's just what you want us to think."

She threw another tomato at him. This one fell short and landed in the grass.

"You're German!" Mrs. Connelly shouted. "You're helping them kill Americans."

Alan looked around. Neighbors were looking out of their windows and stepping out onto their porches. None of them spoke up in his defense.

Did they all believe Mrs. Connelly?

These were his neighbors. They all knew him. How could they think such evil of him? His own daughter had died from the flu and Emily was in the hospital right now trying to fight it off.

Mrs. Connelly pulled another tomato from the bucket and Alan ran. He wasn't going to stand around dodging vegetables until Mrs. Connelly ran out. He sprinted the last hundred feet or so to his house and bounded up the stair to the front door. Behind him, he could still hear Mrs. Connelly screaming at him.

He slammed the door of his house shut and locked it. Then he leaned against the wall and tried to catch his breath with deep gasps.

How dare they! He mourned for their losses. He wasn't trying to harm them.

Alan sat down on the steps and pulled his shoes off, tossing them off to the side. His feet felt heavy.

Right now, all he wanted was sleep. It had been a long day that had now ended in a nightmare. He had only been getting about four hours of sleep a night. It was beginning to catch up with him.

He thought about fixing himself something to eat, but he wasn't hungry. The house was quiet.

Too quiet.

It had once held Anne's laughter and Emily's music.

He staggered upstairs to the bedroom. He looked at himself in the mirror. He looked exhausted and his face was flushed. Neither was a good sign.

Alan fell into the bed and was asleep almost immediately.

FRIDAY, OCTOBER 18, 1918

Alan felt miserable. He had the flu and he blamed Kolas for it. When the man had escaped the police by spitting in Alan's face, the saliva must have infected Alan. Of course, there were probably a dozen other ways he could have been infected, but it was just easier to blame Kolas.

It gave Alan one more reason to want to see Kolas captured.

Now Alan was stuck in his bed alone in his house. He had been tempted to go to the hospital and check himself in, but he didn't want to infect anyone there, especially Emily.

His condition seemed to be holding steady. He wasn't getting any worse for the moment. Alan attributed that to his quick treatment of his symptoms. Now all he wanted was plenty of sleep.

He heard a knock at the door.

"Come in," Alan called.

"It's me, Doc!" Cow called from the first floor.

"I'm in the bedroom."

Alan heard Cow's heavy tread coming up the stairs. The door opened.

"Hi, Doc!" Cow said. He walked into the bedroom smiling broadly.

Alan pushed himself into a sitting position, but he kept his blankets around him.

"Hello, Cow. Are you sure you want to be in here? I've got the flu."

"I know. That's why I'm here. I thought you might need some things. I also needed to tell you something," Cow told him.

"Aren't you afraid of catching the flu?"

Cow shrugged. "I gave up trying to avoid it days ago. I found my own cure."

"What's that?" Alan had heard of many cures for the flu and he wondered which one Cow had chosen to use.

Cow pulled a metal flask out of his back pocket and held it up. He jiggled it and Alan heard the liquid sloshing inside.

"Bourbon?" Alan asked.

"Nothing so fancy. It's whiskey."

"That's not really a cure, you know."

Cow shrugged. "It's as good as anything else that's been used as a cure and it tastes better than quinine. If I'm going to get the flu, I'm going to get it. I have no real idea of how to stop it even if I wanted to try. This helps me control my fear."

Cow sat down in the chair near the bed.

"It's cold in here," he said, glancing at the open window.

"Sorry. I need to keep the room ventilated. I've got four blankets on me so I don't feel it too much. So what brings you by?"

Cow shivered. "I guess I won't be taking off my coat then."

He held up the brown bag he was carrying. He opened it and took out a wrapped sandwich and handed it to Alan. Then he pulled out a small covered crock.

Alan unwrapped the sandwich and lifted the edge of the wheat bread. It was ham and cheese. He bit into it and forced himself to chew, though he didn't feel hungry. He wasn't going to be rude, though and he certainly needed to make sure he didn't starve himself.

Alan opened the crock and inhaled the scent of the tomato soup. It made his stomach rumble. Hopefully, it tasted as good as it smelled.

"I hear that I was right," Cow said.

"Hear?"

Cow pointed to Alan's stomach. "It's pretty loud."

"I haven't been eating much lately. At first, I couldn't hold anything down. Now I'm just too tired to move around much," Alan said.

Cow nodded. "I know. I live alone. I know what it's like when you're sick to have to choose between resting and getting up to make yourself a meal. A lot of times you choose resting."

Alan nodded as he bit into the sandwich. That was exactly how he felt.

"How did you hear about me?" Alan asked.

"I stopped by the hospital to let you know what's happening with Kolas and Helen told me that you were sick."

"Did you catch him?" Alan asked anxiously.

Cow frowned and shook his head. "No, not yet. We can't find him anywhere. If he's still preaching around town, no one is talking about it. We're beginning to ask for him at the hotels and rooming houses. We haven't given up on finding him."

Alan sighed and slumped back into the pillows on his bed.

"I heard your wife was in the hospital. I'm sorry about that. Helen told me to tell you that your wife is doing better. It looks like she's through the worst of it," Cow said.

Alan smiled. "That's good news."

He felt a weight lift off of his shoulders. Emily would be all right.

"The bad news is Dr. Hyatt died last night," Cow said.

Alan's smile fell. Dr. Hyatt was dead? It didn't seem possible. As a doctor, he should have known how best to treat his illness, but he had died just like anyone else could die from this flu.

"He was a good man," Alan said.

Alan ate some more of the sandwich in silence.

"This is very good, Cow. Did you make it yourself?" Alan asked finally.

Cow chuckled. "I figure you have enough problems without me trying to poison you with my food. No, Maxine at Paul's Tavern made up these for you."

"I'll have to thank her."

"I'm surprised there's not a lot more food around here. Ladies around here like to make food for sick people."

"Not if they are German. Our neighbors are polite, but they don't really trust me right now with the war going on."

Alan didn't want to tell Cow how he had been accused of helping the Germans and than no one had come to his aid.

Cow shook his head. "That's too bad. I've always found you to be a nice guy."

"Do you think you will find Kolas?" Alan asked, changing the subject.

Cow shrugged. "If he leaves town, we'll never get a hold of him."

"I don't think he will. He's too committed to spreading the flu here for some reason. He won't leave until the flu does."

Cow pulled an apple out of the bag and bit into it.

"Well, that means we don't have too much time. The flu's dropping off."

"I just hope that doesn't spur him to do something to renew the epidemic," Alan said.

Kolas pressed himself against the wall of the building so that his dark suit would allow him to blend into the dark shadows. He watched the street. A few people hurried along not worried about who else might be walking along. Kolas watched for police in particular. They were searching for him and Kolas didn't intend to allow them to capture him.

When he was sure that no police were nearby, Kolas hurried across Centre Street and moved quickly around to the rear of the brick home. He opened the basement door and slipped inside, shutting the door behind him.

An elderly couple who had died from the flu had owned the house. Because Kolas had helped them take the test, he decided that he could use their empty home as payment for his services. The police were asking for him at the hotels and boarding houses in the city.

On the ground floor, he walked to the parlor and sat down in a comfortable armchair.

A man and woman walked into the parlor from the kitchen. They were followers of Kolas who were assisting him in hiding from the police.

How he wished he could stand once again on the street corners and preach the doctrine of retribution that God was delivering on the world! There were so many people yet to test and save.

"Were you seen?" the man asked.

Kolas shook his head. "No, but the police are still searching. They are even looking in the markets for me now. They must know what I doing there."

"We can continue that work," the woman said. "No one suspects us."

Kolas sighed. "Perhaps, but it is my work and I wish to carry it out."

"You will be doing it again. They can't stop you."

"What about that doctor who was working on a vaccine? Has he had any success?" Kolas asked.

The doctor could not be allowed to be successful. No one must stand in the way of the work of God! Not the doctor. Not the police.

The man shook his head. "No, he gave up the first vaccine. He is working on a second vaccine, but that work has stopped."

"Why?"

"He's got the flu. He is home trying to recover."

155

"Why does he fight God so hard?" Kolas asked.

"It is a personal battle with him. First his daughter died from the flu. Then his wife caught it, but it does not appear she will die. Now he is sick."

"It serves him right for trying to stop us," the woman said. She paused and added, "Can he stop us?"

Kolas rose to his feet. "No one can stop God's work. This Dr. Keener is German. He is an enemy of God and this country. He will be stopped."

"But what can be done if the flu doesn't kill him?" the man asked.

"I will deal with him. He wanted to find me so badly for the police. I will make it possible for him, but he will find out what happens to the enemies of country and God."

SATURDAY, OCTOBER 19, 1918

The insistent knocking at the front door woke Alan from a sound sleep. He moaned and rolled over in his bed. He was finally getting his first good sleep and someone had to go and wake him up.

He felt a little better today at least enough to climb out of bed and answer the door.

"I'm coming!" he called.

It had better not be Cow coming with another meal. Cow had been visiting once a day with food. Alan enjoyed his company, but right now he wanted sleep.

Alan rolled out of bed and put on his slippers and robe. Then he walked slowly down the stairs as the knocking continued. His legs were still weak so he made sure to hold onto the banister for support.

He opened the door and said, "Yes?"

Before Alan could react, the door slammed open, knocking him to the floor. Kolas hurried inside and shut the door behind him.

"You!" Kolas said. "You have fought me every step of the way! I was told that you are German. How is it your people fight both the United States and God? Do you not know God's wrath will not be stopped? Do you not know you only condemn your soul?"

No wonder the police couldn't find Kolas. He looked like a different man. The man's usually neat suit was wrinkled as if he had been sleeping in it for days. His hair was unkempt and sticking out in all directions. His eyes were bloodshot.

"Get out of my house!"

Alan slowly pushed himself to his feet, but he wasn't sure how steady he would remain. He was still sick and weak.

How had Kolas found out what where he lived and what was he doing here?

Kolas crossed his arms over his chest. "I will not leave. You and

157

those like you have the police hunting for me, but you don't realize I can't be stopped. I am doing the work of God. I am God's wrath! The world will repent or perish!"

A flurry of emotions shot through Alan. How dare this man invade his home! He was glad that Emily wasn't here. This man could have been responsible for infecting Anne with his crazy ideas and contaminated apples. The police needed to capture him. What was Kolas going to do to Alan?

"God doesn't want this!" Alan shouted.

"How would you know? I have spoken with God. I have been given my mission by an angel of retribution and I will not fail him," Kolas said.

Alan backed into the living room. Kolas trailed behind him smiling. Good. Alan had an idea that might work to stop Kolas.

He stumbled and went to one knee but then stood back up.

"What are you doing here?" Alan asked.

"I wanted to make sure that you are tested, for I am sure that God will find you wanting and kill you," said Kolas.

Kolas spit into his hands and smeared them with saliva so that they glistened when he held them up. He reached out toward Alan.

Alan jumped backward. As he did, he knocked over the telephone table. He grabbed the small table and threw it at Kolas. It hit Kolas in the chest. He fell with a loud grunt.

While Kolas was getting up, Alan dialed the operator and left the handset on the floor as he turned to face Kolas.

"Your struggles are futile. God's wrath will not be thwarted," Kolas said.

"Leave me alone! You're helping murder people. That's why the police are looking for you!" Alan shouted, hoping the operator was paying attention.

"I murder no one. I only test them. I am God's tool. It is he who finds them wanting and slays them," Kolas said.

"You're no tool for God. You are a snake oil salesman!"

Kolas paused. His eyes went wide and then narrowed as he stared at Alan. "Carson Riley was such a man, but I am Kolas."

"You are Riley!"

Alan backed away toward the kitchen, wondering if he could get a knife from a drawer in time to hold off Kolas.

Kolas shook his hands at the ceiling. "I am Kolas! God tested me as he tests everyone, but I survived. An angel came to me and healed me of my illness so that I might serve him."

Behind Kolas, the door to the house flew open. Cow rushed into the house with his baton held at the ready in his hand.

"Police!" Cow shouted.

Kolas turned to see what was happening. Alan rushed forward and kicked him behind the knees to that Kolas's leg buckled and he fell to the floor.

"Watch his hands, Cow! He was trying to infect me," Alan warned his friend.

Cow walked up to Kolas. Kolas reached out toward him and Cow rapped his knuckles with the baton. Kolas yelled and pulled his hand back, cradling it near his chest.

"I don't think he'll reach his hands out toward anyone soon," Cow said. "Do you have some gloves that we can put on his hands, Doc?" Cow asked.

Alan nodded. He walked unsteadily to the closet and pulled out his winter gloves from the top shelf. They had been a gift from Emily when he had graduated medical school. Alan gave them to Cow, but Cow just tossed them to Kolas.

"You put them on," Cow said.

Kolas whimpered, but he did what Cow asked.

When he was finished, Cow said, "Now I'm going to help you stand up, but if I see you trying to work up any spit, you're going to be missing teeth." Cow held up a clenched fist. "Do you understand what I'm saying to you?"

Kolas nodded. Cow grabbed him under the arm and helped him to his feet.

"Did the operator call you?" Alan asked.

Cow nodded. "She heard your conversation on the open line."

Just as Alan had hoped would happen when he knocked the telephone handset out of place. Operators had been listening in on conversations lately to make sure they were important. Too few operators were reporting to work because of the flu outbreak and the telephone company had asked that the telephone only be used in case of emergency or other important matters. If the operators deemed the calls unimportant, they cut the calls off. They had too much other work to do.

Alan had an idea of some good that might come out of all this.

"Before you take him away, Cow, let me do something," Alan said.

Alan hurried to the closet and pulled out his valise. He opened it up and took out an empty glass syringe.

"What are going to do with that?" Cow asked.

"I want a sample of his blood. He survived the flu. He has an immunity to it. Maybe I can use his blood to create a vaccine that will work for others."

Cow chuckled. "Wouldn't that be ironic?"

"What?"

"Using his blood to heal the people he infected."

Alan grabbed Kolas's arm and straightened it out. Kolas began to struggle, but then he looked at Cow. Cow held up his baton and rested it against the side of Kolas's head. Kolas stopped. Alan slid the needle into Kolas's arm and filled the syringe with Kolas's blood.

"I've got to get to the lab at the hospital," Alan said.

This was the opportunity he had been waiting for. He had a sample from someone who was immune to the flu. Now he could study the blood sample and compare to samples from patients who had died. The differences would be the answer he needed.

Alan hurried to the stairs as fast as his wobbly legs would carry him. He needed to get dressed and get to the hospital laboratory.

"I thought you were still sick."

"I am, but I can't let this wait. I'll manage. It will be worth it. I'll get changed and go in now," Alan told him.

Cow shrugged. "Well, you're the doctor."

Cow hauled Kolas out the door. He put him into the back of the police car.

Thursday,
October 24, 1918

Lorene lay on the cot at the emergency hospital on Washington Street. She burned with a fever, although the window in her room was open. She felt miserable. Would she ever find a way to be free from this flu? Had God finally decided that she needed to die from the flu because she hadn't done what Kolas wanted her to do?

Was God going to kill her because she didn't kill others?

Had she finally failed Kolas's test?

Mrs. Lichtenstein walked in with a small tray in her hands. She sat down next to Lorene's bed and patted Lorene's hand.

"How are you feeling today, dear?" she asked.

"Miserable."

"Well, Dr. Keener has developed a new vaccine that he hopes will work against the flu," the superintendent said. "Would you like to try it?"

"What is it?"

She remembered his last vaccine. All it had done was make her arm sore for two days. She could do without more misery from a worthless vaccine.

"The police captured that street preacher who was trying to spread the flu. Dr. Keener took some of his blood to make this vaccine. It seems the man had developed flu immunities from his own exposure. Dr. Keener's hoping that he was able to capture the immunities in the vaccine."

Kolas captured? Arrested? He had proclaimed himself unstoppable because he was doing God's work. Yet he'd been arrested.

Lorene frowned and held out her arm.

"If it might help, I'll try it."

Mrs. Lichtenstein prepared the syringe.

Cow stopped by to visit Lorene that evening. She was sitting up in her bed and reading the newspaper. He thought, except for being a bit pale, she looked fine.

"I heard you had gotten sick again," Cow said.

She smiled at Cow. "I was, but I don't feel too bad now. My fever broke a little while ago. Now I'm just feeling weak."

He sat down on the low stool near her bed. "Well, that's good news. I suppose you'll be back to work soon."

Lorene nodded. "Dr. Keener's vaccine worked this time."

Cow thought for a moment and shrugged. "Maybe. Maybe not. He's not so sure himself. I don't think vaccines can work that quickly and besides, the flu was already on the decline."

Cow had been disappointed to hear Alan wasn't totally sure the vaccine from Kolas's blood had worked. That would have been the ultimate justice for all the problems Kolas had caused.

"Are you sure?" Lorene asked.

"No, but you can ask Dr. Keener when you see him. He gave the new vaccine to one hundred people. If it works for you, it will work for them, too."

"Where is he?"

Cow grinned. "He's a bit busy right now."

Alan paced the waiting room in the hospital. He was tempted to sneak back to the delivery room, but Helen's stern look warned him not to try it. He was not a doctor right now. He was just another expectant father and she would treat him as such.

What if Anne wasn't strong enough to deliver the baby after having fought the flu? What if the flu had harmed the baby in some way?

He paced even faster. Unable to wait any longer, he headed for the hallway. Helen stepped in front of him to block him.

"I don't think so, Doctor," she said.

"I just want to go to my office," Alan lied.

He needed to get past her. Emily needed him.

"Which would take you right by the delivery room," Helen said.

Alan tried a friendly smile. "You're too suspicious, Helen. I just want to do some work to occupy my mind."

Helen didn't move.

"Just let Dr. Bromwell do his work," she said.

"Why can't I be in there with my wife?" Alan pleaded.

"You'd just be in the way. Let the doctor do his job."

"I'm a doctor."

"You're an expectant father."

Alan sighed and shook his head.

"I'll get even with you for this, Helen," he warned her.

She smiled. "You'll try."

Alan went back to his pacing. He wasn't sure how far he had walked when Dr. Bromwell came out into the waiting room.

"Alan," he said.

Alan hurried over to the older man.

"You have a new son. Both Emily and the baby are doing fine."

Alan's legs felt weak and he had to brace himself against Helen's desk. It wasn't an aftereffect of the flu. It was relief from the tension of not knowing what was happening to Emily.

"Can I see them?" Alan asked.

Dr. Bromwell nodded. "Emily's in room seven. Go on in. I'll have someone bring the baby in in a few minutes."

"Thank you."

Alan felt like cheering. He was a father again! He only wished that Anne could have been around to see her little brother.

FRIDAY, OCTOBER 25, 1918

Alan woke up on Friday morning and just lay in bed. Emily lay next to him asleep and Thomas Michael Keener lay in the bassinet not far from the bed.

Alan took a deep breath and thought *I'm breathing air free of the flu germs.*

The Board of Health was lifting the county ban caused by the Spanish Flu epidemic today, though the city ban was expected to last for another week. Still, the number of new flu cases had almost vanished. The last two patients from the Washington Street Emergency Hospital were going to be moved to Western Maryland Hospital today and the last of emergency hospitals would close down.

Alan had been giving out his vaccine to all the flu patients who were willing to try it. It had taken a few more samples of Carson Riley's blood to make it, but the man didn't have much say in it, not with Cow standing nearby tapping his baton against one hand.

The man was positively crazy. He talked of seeing angels and visions. Sometimes he even talked to the unseen angel while he was sitting alone in his cell. Once he had even called on the angel to strike Alan dead as he drew blood from Riley. Needless to say, Riley was surprised when Alan walked away from him unharmed.

Alan wasn't sure whether his vaccine was helping or not since the flu had already been on the decline throughout the county when he developed the vaccine. The important thing was that it was on the decline and if his vaccine helped speed things up so much the better.

The nightmare was ending.

Alan sighed and went back to sleep.

Lorene watched the last two patients get loaded into the ambulance. She looked over at Calvin who was standing nearby, watching her as if he expected her to collapse.

"I guess I'm out of work now," she said.

Cow shrugged. "I don't know. With the experience you got working through all this, you could probably get a job at one of the city hospitals."

The hospitals were still short staffed because of the nurses who had died from Spanish Flu.

"Not likely. I need formal training," Lorene said.

"Then go get it."

Cow made it sound so simple, but why couldn't she go get it? She had enjoyed nursing. It had taken her mind off her troubles. Her parents would certainly help her go to nursing school if she wanted.

"I think I may try to become a nurse," she mused.

"Lorene..." Cow said.

She turned her attention to Cow. "Yes."

"I was, uh...I wondered, well, I wondered if you might want to go to church with me on Sunday," Cow finally asked.

"Church?"

"I started going to church again because of everything that happened. It made me feel a lot better. I know you were pretty upset about Robert dying, but I thought maybe if you come with me, it might help you feel better, too," he explained.

She stared at him, looking directly into her eyes. Cow didn't look away.

"I would love to go with you, Calvin," she said.

Afterword:
Spanish Flu in
Allegany County

The Spanish Flu began with a cough and muscle aches. It ended in death. Not in every case, but forty million of them ended that way.

In 1918, the world was at war with a deadly enemy. The two battled for about a year until the enemy retreated and hid but not before killing about forty million people or more than seven times the population of Maryland.

It was not World War I that killed all those people. It was the Spanish Flu. It was called Spanish Flu because its first noted appearance was in Spain, but it was simply 1918's flu strain, a strain that happened to be deadly.

The problem with the flu virus is that it mutates fairly easily and you are never sure of how virulent a flu you will wind up with. The SARS scare killed a few hundred people out of a worldwide population of four billion plus. Now imagine the terror people felt in 1918 about a flu that killed two-hundred-thousand times the number killed by SARS in a world that was half as populated.

Spanish Flu killed more people than were killed in World War I and in a shorter time frame, too, yet the war captured the headlines during 1918. Estimates are six-hundred-and-seventy-five-thousand Americans died from the Spanish Flu or ten times more than died in the war.

People had reason to fear for their lives.

Spanish Flu killed more people in one year than the Black Plague did in four years.

Spanish Flu was so devastating that human life span was reduced by ten years in 1918.

After one month in Philadelphia, the flu had killed nearly eleven thousand people, including almost eight hundred people on October 10, 1918.

One physician wrote that patients rapidly "develop the most vicious type of pneumonia that has ever been seen" and later when cyanosis appeared in patients "it is simply a struggle for air until they suffocate." Another doctor said that the influenza patients "died struggling to clear their airways of a blood-tinged froth that sometimes gushed from their mouth and nose."

The reactions at the time were sometimes draconian. Washington, D.C. passed a law that it was illegal to appear outdoors. San Francisco and San Diego forced their citizens to wear gauze masks. Some towns required a signed certificate if someone wanted to enter the town.

In Allegany County, the *Cumberland Evening Times* took little notice of the flu until the end of September. At that time, the article was about the effect of the flu on other places and the problems it was causing.

Then people began to get sick and die in Allegany County.

On October 4, 1918, the Board of Health passed an order closing schools, churches, theaters and dance halls. Streetcars and other public transportation had to travel with windows open. Plus, a person couldn't spit on the street and needed to use a handkerchief when he or she coughed or sneezed. This is because fresh air was believed to be the best defense against Spanish Flu. County Commissioner James McAlpine was the interim health officer at the time and Ralph Rizer signed the order.

The order came too late to help much. All of the obituaries for people who died the day the Board of Health's order was issued died from Spanish Influenza. The same issue of the paper also noted that hospitals were so helpless about treating the flu, they didn't want to risk spreading the flu to other patients who would be susceptible. They asked that flu cases not be brought to the hospitals.

How bad was the flu in Allegany County? The Baltimore and Ohio Railroad had six thousand employees in the county at that time; one thousand of them reported sick with the flu on October 4.

One of the problems with combating the flu was that modern medicine was still in its infancy. People just didn't know much about germ theory let alone viruses, which are even smaller. No real defense or treatment for the flu existed.

Doctors developed crude vaccines or throat gargles by straining blood and mucus from people who had survived the flu. The vaccines were injected into people's arms. The gargles were sprayed in a person's throat. Both had no effect.

On October 5, pool halls and bars were added to the places the Board of Health closed during the epidemic. Drug clerks were becoming overworked trying to fill all of the orders for medicines. They weren't the only ones, either.

One article in the *Cumberland Evening Times* said, "The physicians of the city are having a hard time trying to do justice to their many patients. Three prominent physicians are confined to their homes with the prevailing ailment, hence their patients have to be looked after by other doctors, and the shortage of physicians makes it all the harder for those who are able to make the rounds and also to respond to new calls constantly coming in.

"The department stores, in fact the stores generally, are all hard pushed for help. At one large department store it was stated this morning that they were short some thirty-two clerks."

The doctor problem was one of the insidious ways Spanish Flu worked. It not only sickened a person, requiring them to need medical attention, but it sickened doctors and nurses making them unavailable to treat patients who desperately needed their help.

The *Cumberland Evening Times* wrote, "The number of cases up to and including yesterday which have come under the notice of the physicians total four thousand. This, of course, does not include the cases which have not been attended by any doctors, which would increase the number to a large extent."

On October 7, the city hospitals, Western Maryland (Memorial) and Allegany (Sacred Heart), were afraid to admit flu patients because it might spread to the other patients.

An emergency hospital operated by the Red Cross was opened on the Sprigg property on 28 Washington Street that was owned by the Lowndes family. James W. Thomas who owned the property across the street donated it to serve as a nurses' residence. The hospital was expected to accommodate one hundred patients.

Since the schools were closed because of the Board of Health order, the board of education asked the teachers to volunteer at the hospitals.

Churches like St. Patrick's and Saints Peter and Paul held their services outside to comply with the health order.

The Central YMCA offered its public areas as an emergency hospital.

The physicians created a ward system throughout the city to try and handle the demand for treatment with thinning resources.

By October 8, people began to realize the problem was even worse than the Board of Health thought. First off, influenza was not a disease doctors had to report. It became one after this epidemic. Second, because the doctors were short handed, they weren't filling out the death reports that they should have been. This led to an under reporting of deaths attributable to the flu.

As the number of deaths increased, the shortage extended to gravediggers. The *Cumberland Evening Times* reported, "Several funerals may have to be postponed because grave diggers at Rose Hill cemetery are overtaxed. It was reported this afternoon that orders were in for ten graves to be dug, but one so far had been prepared."

An article in the *Journal of the Alleghenies* read, "Bodies of Frostburg servicemen stationed at Fort Meade were sent back to Frostburg wrapped in blankets and tagged. Their bodies were stored temporarily in the corner house where the Frostburg Legion building now stands. Behind the post office in a carriage house, open doors revealed bodies laid on the floor. At the Durst Funeral Home from October 5 to October 31, 1919, ninety-nine bodies were prepared for the last rites. Those bodies, placed in rough caskets or wooden boxes, were carted to the cemetery and stacked until burial."

The phone company also pleaded for people to only utilize the phones in case of emergency because they were short operators because of the flu.

On October 9, the *Cumberland Evening Times* reported, "It is said that the deaths being recorded are greater than at any other time in the history of the town unless it was in Civil War days when there was a cholera epidemic."

It was also reported in the newspaper that nurses were being overworked. "The hospitals are seriously handicapped in handling cases because so many nurses being ill from influenza. At the Western Maryland, it was stated thirteen nurses were incapacitated and all but three were able to look after patients. At the Allegany Hospital, the situation is almost identical, the nurses who are able to be on duty being worked to the limit."

Things worsened. Twelve people died in one day in Lonaconing. Arrests were made because streetcars traveled with their windows closed.

Coal production in the numerous mines in the George's Creek region fell off because the miners took sick.

The size and colors of wreaths hung on doors of homes indicated who had died in the house.

Some help came with special trains sponsored by the state and federal governments that were traveling hospitals. Emergency hospitals were opened at the B&O YMCA on Virginia Avenue and Laughlin's Hall in Piedmont.

At this point, the B&O Railroad, which had one-thousand workers out earlier now had thirty-five-hundred people – nearly six out of every ten railroad workers in Cumberland – out sick with the flu.

Finally, by October 16, doctors began to report that they were catching up in their case loads. Over the next couple weeks, new cases began to drop off and the hospitals began to empty of flu patients. On October 25, the Board of Health ban was finally lifted.

Because of the problems with reporting, the precise number of Allegany County residents who died from Spanish Influenza is only a range. It appears that four hundred to five hundred residents died of the Spanish Flu during October. That is equivalent to losing a town the size of Barton or Midland in one month.

It is the deadliest plague that has ever struck the world and yet, it remains largely forgotten either through the selective memories of the people who lived through it or because history books remember World War I and not the flu.

Whatever the reason, October 1918 remains the month that the world mourned.

About the Author

James is the author of six other novels. These include the historical novels *Canawlers, Between Rail and River* and *The Rain Man.* His other novels are *Logan's Fire, Beast* and *My Little Angel.* A new young-adult novel *Geoff's Power* is due out in 2006.

He works as a reporter with the *Frederick News-Post* in Frederick, Maryland. Jim has received numerous awards from the Maryland-Delaware-DC Press Association, Associated Press, Maryland State Teachers Association and Community Newspapers Holdings, Inc. for his newspaper writing.

He lives with his wife, Amy, and sons, Ben and Sam, in Gettysburg, PA and is currently at work on his next novel.

If you would like to be kept up to date on new books being published by James or ask him questions, he can be reached by e-mail at jimrada@yahoo.com.

DON'T MISS THESE BOOKS BY JAMES RADA, JR.

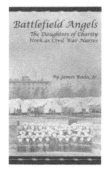

BATTLEFIELD ANGELS: THE DAUGHTERS OF CHARITY WORK AS CIVIL WAR NURSES

The Daughters of Charity were the only trained nurses in the country at the start of the Civil War. They served on the battlefields, in hospitals, on riverboat hospitals, and in prisoner-of-war camps. Learn their stories of pioneering nursing to the wounded and dying on both sides of the war and how it improved nursing and broke down religious bias against Catholics in the U.S.

THE LAST TO FALL: THE 1922 MARCH, BATTLES, & DEATHS OF U.S. MARINES AT GETTYSBURG

In 1922, a quarter of the U.S. Marine Corps marched from Quantico to Gettysburg where they conducted re-enactments of Pickett's Charge for 100,000 spectators. They also conducted modern versions of the battle with tanks, machine guns and airplanes. Two Marines were killed on the battlefield making them the last military deaths on the battlefield.

NO NORTH, NO SOUTH…: THE GRAND REUNION AT THE 50TH ANNIVERSARY OF THE BATTLE OF GETTYSBURG

In 1913, more than 57,000 Civil War veterans returned to Gettysburg for the 50th anniversary of the battle fought there. Confederate and Union veterans alike spent a week on the battlefield reliving old memories and finally bringing peace between the North and the South.

Available wherever books are sold.

172